# BURN WITH ME

## TATUM VALE

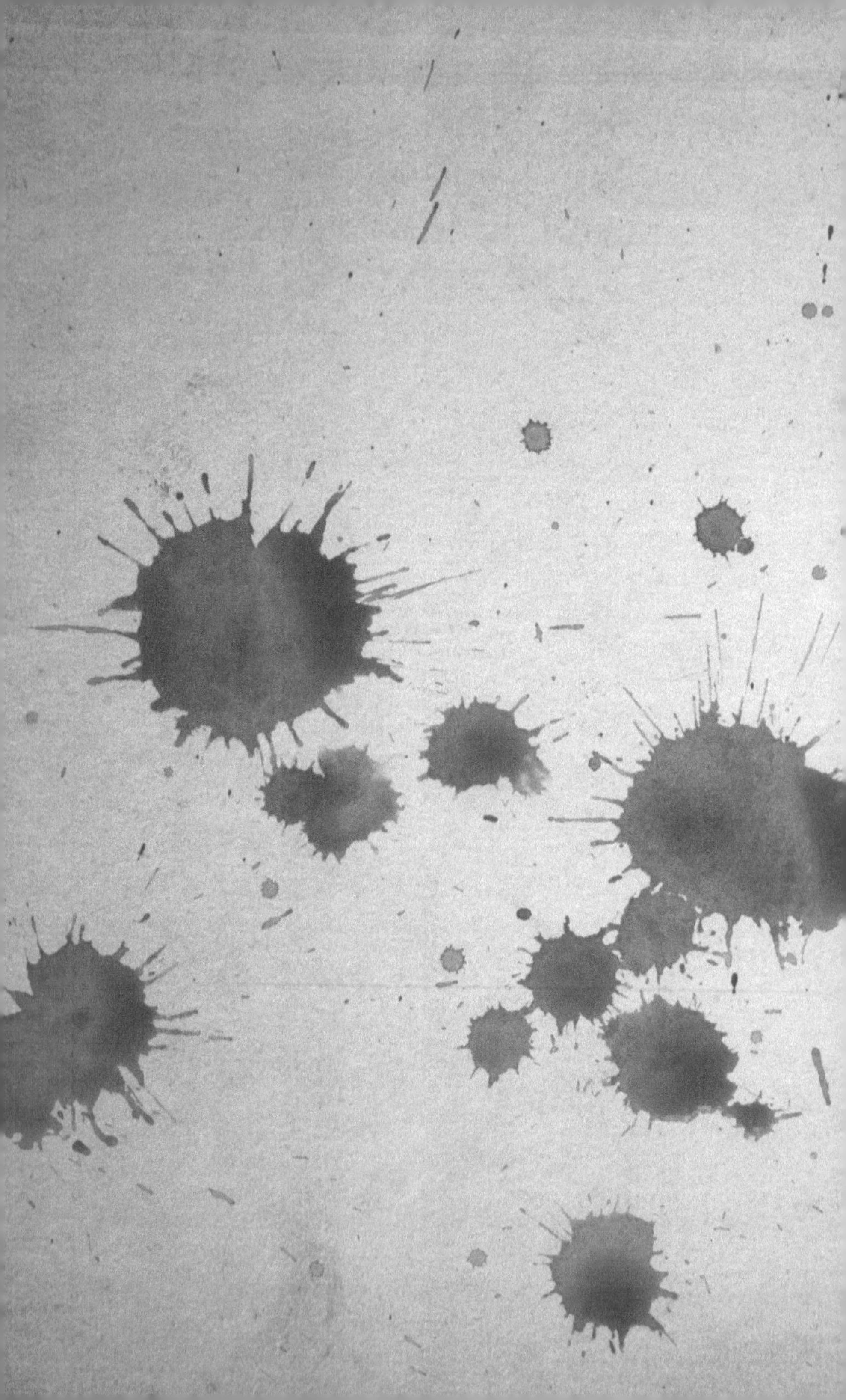

# PLAYLIST

Snuff by Slipknot
Supermassive Black Hole by Muse
Headstrong by Trapt
Shimmer by Fuel
Face Down by The Red Jumpsuit Apparatus
Animal I Have Become by Three Days Grace
Wrong Side of Heaven by Five Finger Death Punch
Gasoline by I Prevail
Riot by Hollywood Undead
Hurt by Johnny Cash
My Immortal by Evanescence
Arsonist's Lullaby by Hozier
I Will Not Bow by Breaking Benjamin
Last Resort by Papa Roach
Second & Sebring by Of Mice & Men

# Author's Note

This is a romantic tragedy in the truest sense. These aren't antiheroes, they're deeply flawed women whose love becomes its own form of violence. I want to be honest about what you're walking into.

The violence is graphic and frequent. Murder, torture, bombings, all depicted in detail. There's death of innocent people, and the main characters are responsible. If you're sensitive to violence, this will be hard to read.

There's explicit sexual content throughout, often intertwined with violence and emotional intensity. It's raw and not always healthy.

One of the main characters struggles with mental health issues including psychiatric hospitalization, self-destructive behavior, and suicidal ideation. There's also grooming and psychological manipulation of a teenage character by an adult.

The family dynamics are toxic, emotional abuse, manipulation, weaponized love. There's substance use as a coping mechanism. And the central relationship is codependent and obsessive in ways that blur devotion and destruction.

The ending is tragic. This is not a happily ever after. If you need your romance to end with hope and survival, this will break your heart.
I've written this story with care, never glorifying the violence or pretending these choices don't have weight. But I won't apologize for writing complicated, messy women who love each other in ways that are beautiful and terrible at once.

If any of this feels like too much, trust your instincts. But if you're here for tragedy and catharsis, for beauty in darkness, thank you for trusting me with your heart.

*For everyone who has ever loved someone so fiercely that the world felt too small to contain it.*
*For the broken ones who found wholeness in another broken soul.*
*For those who chose to burn rather than fade away quietly.*
*This story is yours.*

# PROLOGUE
# NADIA

## THE EDGE OF THE ABYSS

The penthouse windows stretch from floor to ceiling, offering a view of the city that glitters like broken glass scattered across velvet. Moscow sprawls below, indifferent and eternal, its lights bleeding into the darkness. Rain streaks the glass in rivulets, distorting the world beyond into something abstract, something unreal.

I stand at the window, my reflection a ghost superimposed over the cityscape. Blood speckles my white shirt. Not mine. Never mine. My hands are steady, but inside, something has fractured. Something fundamental.

Behind me, the penthouse is a tableau of violence.

Bodies lie where they fell: three men, all dead before they hit the ground. The marble floor is slick with blood, a dark pool spreading slowly toward the white leather furniture. The air smells of copper and gunpowder and expensive cologne. Classical music still plays from hidden speakers, a Chopin nocturne that turns the carnage into something almost beautiful.

Almost.

"You're thinking too much," Kira says.

I don't turn. I can see her reflection in the window, standing in the center of the room like a dancer on a stage.

Wild auburn hair, pale skin painted with arterial spray, green eyes bright with something between madness and euphoria. She's holding a knife, turning it over in her hands, watching the blade catch the light.

"Someone has to," I reply, my voice flat.

She laughs. That sound that makes my chest tighten and my pulse quicken, that sound that means danger and desire in equal measure. "That's your problem, solnyshko. Always thinking. Always calculating. When do you just feel?"

All the time, I think. That's the problem.

I spent fifteen years building walls, constructing myself into something cold and perfect and untouchable. The Black Dahlia. Viktor's most efficient weapon. A woman who could kill without hesitation, without remorse, without leaving a trace.

And then Kira tore through those walls like they were made of paper.

"We need to leave," I say, finally turning from the window. "We have maybe ten minutes before…"

"Before what?" she interrupts, spreading her arms wide. "Before they find the bodies? Before Viktor sends someone else to clean up his mess? Before the world ends?" She spins in a slow circle, her boots squelching in blood. "Let it burn, Nadia. Let it all burn."

"That's not a plan."

"Plans are boring." She steps closer, closing the distance between us with that predatory grace that makes my breath catch. "You know what's not boring? This. Us. Right now, in this moment, with the world falling apart around us."

She's close enough now that I can smell her. Sweat and smoke and something darker, something intoxicating. She reaches up, her blood-stained fingers tracing the line of my jaw, and I should pull away. Should maintain distance, control, the professional detachment that kept me alive this long.

Instead, I lean into the touch.

"You're going to get us killed," I whisper.

She smiles, fearless and radiant. "Maybe. But at least you'll feel something when you die."

Our lips meet in a kiss that tastes like violence and desperation, like the end of everything. My hands find her waist, pulling her closer, blood-slick fingers gripping the torn fabric of her dress.

She moans into my mouth, pressing her body flush against mine. Her hands tangle in my hair, pulling hard enough to hurt, and I respond by backing her against the blood-spattered window.

"We don't have time," I gasp against her lips.

"Then make it quick," she breathes, her hand sliding down my stomach.

My hand finds its way beneath her dress, fingers sliding between her thighs. She's already wet, desperate, her hips rocking forward to meet my touch.

"God, you're perfect," I whisper, working my fingers inside as she bites down on my shoulder to muffle her cries.

It's fast, frantic, surrounded by death and the sound of approaching sirens. She comes with my name broken on her lips, her body shaking, tears mixing with blood on her cheeks.

When we break apart, both breathing hard, she rests her forehead against mine.

"Do you believe in anything?" she whispers. "After, I mean."

I consider the question. I used to believe in nothing. That death was just the end. Darkness. Silence.

"I want to believe there's something," I admit. "A garden, maybe. With black dahlias. And you. And peace."

Her eyes fill with tears. "That sounds perfect."

"What about you?"

"I hope we get to pay for what we've done," she says quietly. "For all of them. But after... maybe then we get something clean. Somewhere we can just be two people who love each other." she says quietly.

I pull her closer. "I'll find you. In whatever comes next. Even if I have to burn through heaven and hell."

She laughs through her tears. "Promise?"

"Promise."

"Run away with me," she murmurs.

"Where would we go?"

"Anywhere. Everywhere. Does it matter?" Her eyes search mine, suddenly vulnerable in a way that makes my heart ache. "We could disappear. Become ghosts. Be free."

I want to say yes. The word is right there, trembling on my lips. Yes, let's run. Yes, let's burn it all down. Yes, I choose you over everything.

But I'm the Black Dahlia. I'm Viktor's creation. I'm a weapon, not a woman.

Aren't I?

"Kira…"

The sound of footsteps in the hallway cuts me off. Heavy boots. Multiple people. We're out of time.

Her expression shifts instantly, the vulnerability vanishing behind a mask of manic energy. She grabs my hand, squeezes once, and grins. "Plan B?"

"We don't have a Plan B."

"Then we improvise." She pulls me toward the balcony. "Do you trust me?"

It's a ridiculous question. She's chaos incarnate, a force of nature that destroys everything it touches. Trusting her is suicide.

But when I look at her, wild and fearless, I realize something terrifying: I do trust her. Against all logic, against all training, against every instinct that kept me alive for fifteen years, I trust Kira Sokolov completely.

"Yes," I say.

Her smile could light the city on fire.

"Then jump."

# CHAPTER ONE
# NADIA

## THE BLACK DAHLIA

### THREE WEEKS EARLIER

The bass pulses through the Velvet Room like a second heartbeat, drowning out everything except the throb of bodies and the clink of expensive glasses. I move through the crowd like smoke, present but intangible, my black dress absorbing the neon lights that paint the club in shades of crimson and violet. No one looks at me twice. That's the point.

I learned long ago that invisibility is a choice, a discipline. Keep your shoulders relaxed. Don't meet anyone's eyes. Move with the rhythm of the room, not against it. Become part of the scenery until the moment you need to be the storm.

My targets sit in the VIP booth at the back, elevated above the dance floor like kings surveying their kingdom. Two syndicate lieutenants: Dmitri Volkov and his cousin Gregor. They're laughing, heads thrown back, surrounded by women who touch them with practiced affection and hollow eyes. The table between them is littered with champagne bottles, ashtrays, and the careless confidence of men who believe themselves untouchable.

Everyone bleeds, Viktor's voice echoes in my mind. The trick is making them believe they won't until it's too late.

I check my watch. Eleven forty-seven. Thirteen minutes until the shift change for security. Twelve minutes until Dmitri excuses himself for his habitual trip to the restroom. Cocaine and ego, a reliable combination.

I drift toward the bar, order a vodka I won't drink, and wait. My pulse remains steady; my breathing controlled. This is the part I'm good at: the stillness before violence, the cold clarity that comes when everything else falls away. Some people meditate. I kill.

At eleven fifty-three, Dmitri rises from the booth, adjusting his suit jacket. He says something to Gregor that makes the other man laugh, then heads toward the back hallway where the restrooms are. I set down my glass and follow.

The hallway is dimmer, quieter; the music muffled by velvet-lined walls. Dmitri pushes into the men's room without looking back. Arrogant. Sloppy. Fatal.

I count to fifteen, then slip inside.

Dmitri is at the sink, bent over the marble counter, a rolled hundred-dollar bill in one hand and a small mirror in the other. The white powder forms a neat line. He doesn't hear me approach, not until my hand is already around his throat and the garrote wire is biting into his skin.

His eyes bulge. He tries to scream, but the wire cuts off his air. His hands claw at my arms, desperate, animal. I hold firm, my face expressionless, watching his reflection in the mirror as the life drains from his eyes.

It takes forty-three seconds. I count every single one.

When his body goes limp, I lower him gently to the floor, arrange him against the wall as if he'd simply passed out. Then I reach into my jacket and withdraw a single black dahlia, its petals dark as ink, and tuck it into his shirt pocket.

"A flower for the dead," I murmur.

I wash my hands and check my reflection. No blood, no sign of struggle. I walk out.

Back in the main room, Gregor is still laughing, still drinking, still alive. For now. I circle the booth, noting the two bodyguards flanking it, the angle of the security cameras, and the nearest exit. I slip a small vial from my purse. Clear liquid, tasteless, fatal within minutes, and approach the booth from the side where the waitress is preparing another round of drinks.

"Let me help you with that," I say smoothly, taking the tray with a practiced smile.

The waitress, harried and grateful, doesn't question it.

I move through the VIP section, setting drinks down with the efficiency of someone who belongs there. When I place Gregor's glass in front of him, our eyes meet for half a second. He smiles at me, a predator's smile, and I smile back.

You'll be dead before you finish that drink, I think, and turn away.

I'm halfway to the exit when the screaming starts. Someone has found Dmitri. The music cuts off abruptly, replaced by shouts and the thunder of footsteps. I don't run…running draws attention. I walk, calm and unhurried, out the front door and into the rain-slicked street.

Behind me, sirens begin to wail.

THE SAFE HOUSE IS A TWENTY-MINUTE DRIVE ACROSS THE city, a nondescript apartment in a building that asks no questions. I let myself in, lock the door behind me, and finally allowing myself to breathe.

My hands are steady as I strip off my dress, my heels, the wig I wore to change my silhouette. I stand in front of the bathroom mirror, studying my reflection. Pale skin, gray eyes like winter frost, the faint scar along my collarbone from a job that went wrong three years ago.

I am the blade, I tell myself. They'll never see the cut until it's too late.

But tonight, for the first time in a long time, the words feel hollow.

I shower, washing away the sweat and the scent of the club, and dress in simple black pants and a tank top. Then I sit at the small kitchen table and open the manila folder Viktor gave me earlier that evening.

The dossier is thin but thorough. Photographs, surveillance reports, psychological profiles. And at the center of it all, a face that stops me cold.

Kira Sokolov.

Wild green eyes, pale skin, dark auburn hair cut in a choppy, uneven style. She's laughing in one photo, burning a stack of cash in another, kissing a woman in a third. Every image radiates chaos, beauty, danger.

I flip through the pages, reading quickly. Estranged daughter of the Sokolov crime family. History of psychiatric hospitalization. Known for erratic behavior, violence, and a complete disregard for consequences. Considered extremely dangerous.

Viktor's note is clipped to the last page: Eliminate her. No witnesses. No mistakes.

I stare at the photograph, at those eyes that seem to look directly through the camera and into me.

"What's your weakness?" I murmur.

As if in answer, my phone buzzes. A single text from an unknown number.

Catch me if you can. - K

My breath catches. I look around the apartment, suddenly

aware of how exposed I am. How did she get my number? How does she know?

I type a response, then delete it. Then type another. Delete that too.

Finally, I set the phone down and smile. A small, dangerous smile that no one is there to see.

So she knows I'm coming, I think. Good.

I reach for the black dahlia sitting in a glass of water on the windowsill, the one I keep for myself, a reminder of what I am, and twirl it between my fingers.

The hunt has begun.

And for the first time in years, I feel something other than emptiness.

I feel alive.

# CHAPTER TWO
# KIRA

## THE SOKOLOV ESTATE

I know she's here.

The Angel. The Black Dahlia. Viktor's perfect little killing machine. I can feel her presence like static electricity on my skin, that delicious anticipation of knowing death is circling closer.

Good. I've been so fucking bored.

The Sokolov estate sprawls around me like a mausoleum, all wrought-iron gates and manicured gardens, old money whispering its lies. I hate this place. Hate the portraits of dead ancestors judging from the walls, hate the crystal chandeliers that cost more than human lives, hate the men in expensive suits conducting business under the guise of celebration.

Most of all, I hate that they summoned me back. Like I'm a dog, still theirs to command.

Spoiler alert: I'm not.

I stand in front of my bedroom mirror, studying my reflection. The dress they sent me is ridiculous. Some designer thing that probably cost thousands. I took scissors to it an hour ago. Now it looks like something beautiful that survived an accident. Perfect.

My makeup is smudged deliberately: dark eyeliner bleeding down my cheeks like war paint. My hair is a choppy mess because I cut it myself last week with kitchen shears while having a particularly inspired breakdown.

I look exactly like what I am: a disaster in designer clothes. Beautiful.

My phone buzzes. A text from an unknown number, but I know who it is. I've been texting her for days, watching her try to figure out how I got her information. It's adorable, really. She thinks she's the hunter.

She has no idea I've been hunting her right back.

The text reads:

> I'm in position. Stay visible.

I laugh out loud. "In position." Like this is just another job for her. Like I'm just another target.

Oh, Angel. You have no idea what you've walked into.

I slip my phone into my bra because the dress doesn't have pockets. Of course it doesn't. I head downstairs, time to put on a show.

The party is exactly what I expected: a gathering of monsters pretending to be civilized. Men who've ordered executions while discussing wine vintages. Women who've buried bodies wearing pearls and Chanel. My family.

I grab a champagne flute from a passing waiter and drain it in one go. Then I grab another.

"Kira." My stepmother's voice cuts through the noise like a blade. "You're making a scene."

I turn to face her, elegant, cold-eyed, the woman who taught me that love is just another weapon. She's wearing that expression, the one that says I'm an embarrassment she's learned to tolerate.

"Stepmother." I raise my glass in a mock salute. "You look murderous tonight. New Botox?"

Her smile doesn't reach her eyes. "Your father wants to see you."

"I'm sure he does. Tell him I'm busy."

"Kira…"

"Tell him," I interrupt, my voice dropping to something dangerous, "that I'm not his trained dog anymore. If he wants to talk to me, he can come find me himself."

I walk away before she can respond, moving through the crowd with deliberate provocation. I touch shoulders, whisper in ears, leave chaos in my wake. It's what I'm good at.

And all the while, I'm searching. Looking for her.

The Angel.

I find her by the windows, pretending to admire the view. She's dressed in emerald silk that clings to her curves, her dark hair swept up elegantly. She looks like money, like power, like someone who belongs here.

But I can see through the disguise. I can see the predator beneath the pretty dress, the killer hiding behind the champagne glass.

There you are.

Our eyes meet across the crowded room, and I feel it…that electric jolt of recognition. She sees me. Really sees me. Not the crazy daughter, not the family embarrassment, not the broken toy everyone wants to fix or discard.

She sees the monster.

And she doesn't flinch.

I smile at her, slow and dangerous, and watch her jaw tighten. Watch her hand move instinctively toward her thigh where I know she's hiding a weapon.

Yes. This is going to be fun.

I make my way outside to the gardens, needing air, needing space from all these people who look at me like I'm a bomb waiting to explode.

They're not wrong.

That's when I see it: my father's favorite statue. Some Greek god or another, marble and expensive and utterly meaningless. He loves it because it represents "classical beauty" or some bullshit like that.

The sledgehammer is leaning against the garden shed. Probably left by one of the groundskeepers.

I pick it up. It's heavy, solid, perfect.

This is a terrible idea, a small voice in my head whispers.

I know, I think back. That's why I'm doing it.

The first swing feels incredible. The marble cracks, chunks flying. The second swing is even better. By the third, I'm laughing, wild and free, as the statue crumbles into rubble.

The crowd gathers. I can hear them gasping, muttering, probably calling me crazy. My father emerges, his face purple with rage.

"You ungrateful little…" he starts.

"Psychopath?" I finish brightly, turning to face him with the sledgehammer still in my hands. "Lunatic? Disappointment? Come on, Papa, you can do better than that. You've had years to practice."

"Get inside," he growls. "Now."

"Or what? You'll lock me up again? Send me back to the nice doctors with their pills and their padded rooms?" I take a step closer to him, fearless and reckless. "I'm done being your dirty little secret."

He raises his hand, and for a moment, I think he might actually hit me in front of all these witnesses. Part of me wants him to. Part of me wants to see what happens when the mask finally drops completely.

But my stepmother moves between us, her voice low and venomous. "Enough. Both of you."

She turns to me, and the look she gives me is colder than any violence. "Go to your room. We'll discuss this later."

The laughter dies in my throat. For just a moment, something vulnerable flashes through me, something that feels like pain, like the girl who just wanted her to love her.

Then the mask slams back into place, and I grin.

"Yes," I say with exaggerated sweetness.

I drop the sledgehammer, letting it thud against the grass, and turn to leave.

That's when my eyes find hers again.

The Angel. The assassin. The woman who's here to kill me.

She's watching me with an expression I can't quite read. No disgust. Not pity. Something else. Something that looks almost like… recognition?

Time seems to slow down. The world narrows to just us. Her gray eyes lock with my green ones, the space between us charged with something I don't have a name for.

I smile at her, not the wild grin from before, but something more intimate. Like we're sharing a secret.

I know who you are. I know why you're here. And I can't wait to see what you do about it.

Then I walk away, disappearing into the mansion, leaving her standing there in the garden with all the other predators.

BACK IN MY ROOM, I LOCK THE DOOR AND LEAN AGAINST IT, breathing hard. My heart is racing, adrenaline singing through my veins.

She's here. She's actually here.

Viktor sent his best weapon to eliminate me, and instead of fear, all I feel is… excitement. Anticipation. That delicious edge of danger that makes me feel alive.

I cross to my bed, pull out the sketchbook I keep hidden under the mattress. It's filled with drawings: flowers with teeth, bodies twisted in impossible positions, a woman drowning in black water.

And on the last page, sketched from memory: her.

The Angel.

I've been drawing her for weeks, ever since I first learned

Viktor was sending someone. I researched her, studied her work, and fell a little in love with the artistry of her kills. The black dahlias she leaves behind. The precision. The ritual.

She thinks murder can be art. So do I.

My phone buzzes. Another text from her:

Your room. Ten minutes.

I laugh, delighted. She's not even trying to be subtle anymore.

Good. I'm tired of subtlety.

I position myself on the bed, sketchbook in my lap, and wait. The music playing from my speakers is loud, something angry and distorted, all screaming guitars. I want her to know I heard her coming. I want her to know this is a choice.

The door opens.

She slips inside, closing it behind her with barely a sound. In the dim light of my room, surrounded by my art and my chaos, she looks even more dangerous than she did downstairs.

I look up at her, and that smile returns, the one that promises trouble.

"I was wondering when you'd come find me," I say.

She doesn't move from the door, her hand near her weapon. "How did you..."

"Know you were here?" I set down my sketchbook and stand, moving closer. "Please. I've been waiting for Viktor to send someone. I'm surprised it took him this long."

I watch her calculate, her mind racing behind those cold gray eyes. Her cover is blown. The mission is compromised. She should abort, extract, and report back.

But she doesn't move.

"You're the Black Dahlia, aren't you?" I continue, taking another step closer. "Viktor's perfect little assassin. I've heard stories about you." I tilt my head, studying her like she's a puzzle I'm dying to solve. "They say you're cold. Efficient. That you kill without feeling anything."

"They're right," she says, her voice steady despite the way I can see her pulse jumping in her throat.

"Are they?" I'm close enough now that I can see the gold flecks in her gray eyes, can smell her perfume. Something expensive and subtle. "Because right now, you look like you're feeling a lot."

I reach out, my fingers brushing against her wrist, and it's like touching a live wire. Every nerve in my body lights up, screaming danger and desire in equal measure.

"So," I murmur, my lips curving into a smile that's pure temptation. "Are you going to kill me? Or are you going to kiss me?"

I watch her struggle with it: the training, the mission, the carefully constructed walls. I watch her expression shift, her control start to crack.

Then she grabs my wrist, spins me around, and pins me against the wall.

"I haven't decided yet," she whispers against my ear, and the sound sends shivers down my spine.

I laugh, breathless and delighted. "Good. I like surprises."

And in that moment, I realized with perfect, terrifying clarity that I'm in trouble.

Deep, inescapable trouble.

The mission has just become infinitely more complicated, her face says.

Good, mine answers back. I was getting bored with simple things.

# CHAPTER THREE

# NADIA

## ART GALLERY STALK

The gallery is all white walls and cold light, the kind of sterile space that makes violence feel impossible. Which is exactly why I like it. Clean lines. Clear sightlines. Nowhere to hide, which means I can see everything.

I stand in front of a massive canvas, slashes of red and black that might be rage or passion or both, and watch Kira work the room.

Work is the right word. She moves through the crowd like a conductor leading an orchestra of chaos, each gesture deliberate, each laugh calculated to provoke. She wears a blood-red dress that clings to her curves, her hair wild and artfully disheveled, dark lipstick making her mouth look like a wound.

She's magnetic. Dangerous. Beautiful in the way a fire is beautiful, right before it burns your house down.

I sip champagne; I don't taste and listen.

"Darling, this piece is devastating," she says to a man in an expensive suit, her hand trailing along his arm. "Don't you think? All that violence, barely contained. Like it's going to leap off the canvas and devour us."

The man laughs nervously. Her smile sharpens.

"I'm Kira Sokolov," she says, extending her hand. "And you are?"

"Artem Volkov," the man replies, taking her hand. His eyes travel down her body with the subtlety of a sledgehammer.

My jaw clenches. My hand tightens around my glass.

Volkov. One of Viktor's competitors. What is she doing with him?

"Volkov," she purrs. "How delicious. Your family and mine have such a…complicated history."

"We could simplify it," Artem says, leaning closer. "Over drinks, perhaps?"

She laughs, that bright, sharp sound that makes my pulse quicken. "Perhaps. But I'm afraid I'm already spoken for tonight."

Her eyes flick across the room, landing directly on me.

Shit.

I don't move, don't react, but my heart hammers against my ribs. She holds my gaze for three seconds, an eternity. Then turns back to Artem with a dismissive smile.

"Another time," she says, and walks away, leaving him standing there like a man who's just been slapped.

I set down my glass and follow.

The gallery has a back corridor, dimly lit, lined with storage rooms and staff offices. I move silently, tracking her footsteps, the click of her heels on polished concrete.

I find her in a small viewing room, standing in front of a painting of a woman drowning in black water, her mouth open in a silent scream.

"You're not very good at being invisible," she says without turning around.

I stop in the doorway. "You knew I was following you."

"I've known you were following me for three days." She turns, leaning against the wall, arms crossed. "You're good, I'll give you that. But I'm better at being watched."

"Is that what you want? To be watched?"

Her smile is slow, predatory. "I want to be seen. There's a difference."

She pushes off the wall and walks closer, each step deliberate. My hand moves instinctively toward the knife hidden at my hip, but I don't draw it.

"What were you doing with Volkov?" I ask.

"Jealous already?" Her eyes glitter with amusement. "We haven't even had our first date."

"This isn't a game."

"Everything's a game." She stops inches away, close enough that I can smell her perfume, something dark and sweet, like night-blooming flowers and gasoline. "The question is whether you're playing to win or playing not to lose."

"I don't lose."

"Neither do I." Her hand slides up my chest, fingers playing with the collar of my shirt. "So what happens when we're both too stubborn to surrender?"

My breath catches. Every instinct screams at me to step back, to maintain distance, to remember that this woman is a target, not a temptation.

Instead, I grab her wrist and spin her around, pinning her against the wall. The painting of the drowning woman watches us with dead eyes.

"You're playing a dangerous game," I whisper against her ear.

She laughs, breathless and delighted. "Finally. I was beginning to think you were all ice and no fire."

"Answer my question. What were you doing with Volkov?"

"Gathering information. Making him think I'm an asset." She turns her head, our faces inches apart. "He thinks he can use me against my family. He's wrong, of course. But it's fun to let him believe it."

"And what about me? What do you think you can use me for?"

Her expression shifts, the manic energy fading into something quieter, more genuine. "I don't want to use you. I want to know you."

"You don't know my name."

"Don't I?" She smiles. "Nadia Morozova. Age thirty-two. Orphaned at seven. Recruited by Viktor Kuznetsov at sixteen. Twenty-three confirmed kills, though the real number is probably closer to forty. You live alone. You don't have friends. You leave a black dahlia on every body because you think ritual makes murder into art."

My grip tightens. "How…"

"I told you. I've been waiting for Viktor to send someone." Her eyes search mine. "I just didn't expect it to be you. I didn't expect you to be…this."

"What's this?"

"Real." Her voice drops to a whisper. "Everyone else in my life is a ghost or a liar. But you…you're solid. Dangerous. Alive. I can feel it."

I should pull away. Should complete the mission. Should do what Viktor trained me to do.

But she's looking at me like I'm the only real thing in a world of shadows, and I realize with terrifying clarity that I feel the same way.

"This is a mistake," I say.

"Probably." Her lips curve into a smile. "But don't you want to see what happens?"

Before I can answer, voices echo from the main gallery. Security, maybe, or other guests wandering too close.

I release her and step back. "We can't do this here."

"Then where?" She straightens her dress, her expression shifting back to that manic brightness. "Your place? Mine? A dark alley? I'm flexible."

"Nowhere. This ends now."

"Liar." She walks to the door, then pauses, looking back over her shoulder. "You'll come find me again. You won't be able to help yourself."

I can already feel the invisible thread between us pulling taut, a promise neither of us will break.

I LEAVE THE GALLERY TEN MINUTES LATER, MOVING through the crowd like smoke. Outside, the city is alive with light and noise, but I barely notice. My mind is replaying the conversation, the way she looked at me, the way my pulse quickened when she touched my wrist.

She knows too much. She's a liability. I should eliminate her now, before things get more complicated.

But the thought dies as quickly as it forms. I stare at my hands, stained with the invisible blood of dozens, and shudder at the thought of her throat beneath them.

I pull out my phone and text Viktor.

NADIA:

Need more time. Target is more complicated than anticipated.

His response comes immediately.

VIKTOR:

You have 48 hours. No more delays.

I stare at the message, then delete it. Forty-eight hours. Two days to decide whether to kill Kira or…

Or what? Run away with her? Burn down the world together? That's insane.

But as I walk through the rain-slicked streets, I realize something that terrifies me more than any mission ever has: I want to find out.

I want to see what happens when two people who are supposed to destroy each other choose something else instead.

The next morning, I wake to find a package outside my apartment door. No return address. No note.

Inside is a single black dahlia and a photograph.

The photograph shows me at the gallery, standing before the red-and-black painting, my face caught in profile. I look focused, dangerous, beautiful.

On the back, written in red ink:

*I see you too. -K*

I hold the photograph for a long time, tracing the line of my own jaw, the set of my shoulders. She captured something in that image, something I've never seen in myself before.

I look alive. I look like I matter.

This is a mistake, I tell myself again.

But I tuck the photograph into my jacket pocket anyway, right next to my knife.

The hunt is still on. But now, I'm not sure who's hunting whom.

# CHAPTER FOUR
## KIRA

### SYNDICATE GALA

I know this is a trap.

The Volkov estate glitters like a jewel box, every window blazing with light, music spilling into the manicured gardens. It's beautiful in that soulless way expensive things are, perfect and hollow and utterly lifeless.

Just like the people inside.

The invitation arrived this morning on cream-colored cardstock: The Volkov family requests the honor of your presence… Blah blah blah, alliance between families, celebration of unity, all the pretty lies we tell ourselves.

But I know what this really is. It's a stage. A trap. A test.

And I wouldn't miss it for the world.

I'm wearing blood-red, a dress that cost more than most people make in a month, fitted perfectly, with a slit that runs dangerously high up my thigh. My hair is wild as always, dark makeup making my eyes look enormous.

The security guard at the entrance barely glances at my invitation before waving me through. Sloppy. My family would never be this careless.

Then again, my family is currently trying to decide whether to kill me or use me. The Volkovs have already made up their minds.

Inside, the gala is exactly what I expected. A gathering of predators in designer suits, their wives and mistresses in gowns that cost more than human lives. Everyone is smiling, laughing, and conducting business under the guise of celebration.

I grab champagne from a passing waiter and scan the crowd.

Looking for her.

I know she's here. I can feel her presence like static electricity on my skin, that delicious anticipation of knowing the Angel is circling closer.

There.

She stands near the windows in midnight blue silk that hugs her body like a second skin. Her hair is loose for once, falling in dark waves over her shoulders. She looks like money, like power, like someone who belongs in this world of predators.

But I can see, her. I see the blade beneath the beauty.

Our eyes meet across the crowded ballroom, and I feel that electric jolt again. Recognition. Want. Danger.

I smile at her, slow and dangerous, and watch her jaw tighten.

God, I want to make her lose control.

The night drags on. I play my part. Flirting with Artem Volkov, laughing at jokes that aren't funny, touching arms and whispering in ears. All the while, I can feel Nadia watching me.

Jealous yet, Angel?

At midnight, the lights dim. A spotlight illuminates the center of the ballroom. Artem steps onto the stage, microphone in hand.

"Ladies and gentlemen," he says, his voice smooth as oil. "Thank you for joining us tonight. As you know, this gala celebrates the alliance between our families: the Volkovs and the Sokolovs…"

I tune him out. I know what's coming. They're going to

parade me around like a prize, like proof that the families are united, like I'm something they own.

Fuck that.

"And to honor this alliance," Artem continues, "I'd like to invite someone very special to join me. A woman who embodies the beauty and strength of the Sokolov family. Kira Sokolov."

The spotlight swings to find me. I stand frozen for a moment, my smile fixed in place, then walk to the stage.

Time to burn it all down.

Artem takes my hand, kisses it, pulls me close. "A toast," he says, raising his glass. "To new beginnings. To family. To…"

I grab the microphone from his hand.

"To lies," I say, my voice ringing through the ballroom. "To pretty words that mean nothing. To alliances built on blood and broken promises."

The room goes silent. Artem's smile falters.

"Kira…" he starts.

"Did you really think I'd play along?" I ask, looking directly at him. "Did you think I'd smile and nod and let you parade me around like a trophy? Like I'm some prize you won for being born into the right family?"

I can see my stepmother moving toward the stage, her face pale with fury. Security guards shift, hands moving toward weapons.

But I'm not finished.

"I'm not here to celebrate," I say, my eyes scanning the crowd until they find Nadia's. "I'm here to make a confession. There's someone in this room tonight who came to kill me. An assassin. The best in the city, they say. The Black Dahlia."

Gasps ripple through the crowd. Hands move to concealed weapons. Nadia doesn't move, doesn't react, but I can see her pulse jumping in her throat.

Come on, Angel. Let's see what you do.

"And I want you to know," I continue, my voice dropping

to something almost intimate despite the microphone, "that I've been waiting for her. That I want her to try."

I raise my glass. "A toast. To the Angel in the shadows. Come find me."

Then I throw the glass against the wall, shattering it, and walk off the stage.

Chaos erupts. Security swarms. Guests shout questions and accusations. Artem stands on the stage, stunned and furious.

And I disappear into the crowd, heading toward the garden doors.

Your move, Nadia.

THE GARDENS ARE QUIETER, DARKER, LIT ONLY BY STRINGS of lights and the glow from the mansion. I sit on the edge of the fountain, trailing my fingers through the water, waiting.

I know she'll come. She won't be able to help herself.

Footsteps behind me. Silent, controlled. I don't turn around.

"I was beginning to think you wouldn't come," I say.

"What was that? In there?" Her voice is tight with controlled anger.

"The truth." I turn to face her. "I'm tired of pretending. Tired of playing their games."

"So you decided to play a different game? One where you get us both killed?"

"Maybe." I stand, walking closer. "Or maybe I wanted to see if you'd come, anyway. If you'd risk it."

"I'm here to kill you."

"I know." I stop inches away, close enough that she can smell my perfume. "So why haven't you?"

It's a good question. She could do it right now. One quick strike, and it would be over.

But her hand stays at her side.

"You're making this complicated," she says.

"Good." I step closer. "I like complicated."

Before she can respond, gunfire erupts from the mansion. Screams. The sound of breaking glass.

We both turn toward the noise. Through the windows, I can see figures moving, fighting. More gunfire.

What the hell?

A man bursts through the garden doors, gun raised. He wears a mask, but I can tell he's a professional. Another assassin.

He sees us and fires.

Nadia moves on instinct, tackling me to the ground as bullets tear through the air where we were standing. We roll behind the fountain, and she's already drawing her knife.

"Stay down," she hisses.

"Like hell," I reply, pulling a small pistol from my thigh holster.

The assassin advances, firing steadily. Stone chips fly from the fountain. Water sprays from bullet holes.

Nadia moves first. Low and fast, knife leading. The assassin swings his gun toward her, but she's already inside his guard. I fire twice from behind the fountain.

The assassin drops.

Nadia stands over him, breathing hard, blood on her hands. More footsteps, more gunfire from the mansion.

"We need to move," she says.

I'm already on my feet, gun still raised. "Together?"

She looks at me, really looks at me and I see the moment she makes her choice.

"Together."

WE RUN THROUGH THE FOREST, THE PINE TREES THICK AND dark around us. This is old Moscow, the part tourists never see. Where Stalin's dacha once stood, where the elite used to summer before the world changed.

The paths are narrow, winding, and easy to get lost in. But I know them. I've run them a hundred times, memorized every turn, every hiding spot.

Behind us, dogs bark. Flashlights cut through the trees. But they're city men, used to concrete and cars. The forest is ours. Behind us, the Volkov estate has become a war zone. Whoever attacked brought an army.

"The garage," I gasp, pointing. "There's a car."

We reach it, find a black Mercedes with keys in the ignition. We climb in, Nadia behind the wheel, and tear out of the garage as more gunfire erupts behind us.

The gates are closed, but Nadia doesn't slow down. She floors the accelerator, and the Mercedes smashes through the wrought iron, metal screaming.

Then we're on the road, the estate shrinking in the rearview mirror.

I'm laughing. Breathless, manic, my heart racing with adrenaline. "That was incredible."

Nadia's hands are white-knuckled on the steering wheel. Her mind is clearly trying to process what just happened. She saved me. Fought beside me. Ran with me.

Her face is a battlefield of emotions, regret warring with desire. She stares straight ahead, knuckles white on the steering wheel.

"Where to now?" I ask, my voice still breathless from our escape.

The silence stretches between us. Her jaw clenches, then releases. "I need to stop," she finally says, voice low and rough.

"Stop? We can't..."

"Now." The word comes out like a growl, her gaze finally

meeting mine,pupils blown wide, something primal lurking there.

She jerks the wheel suddenly, tires squealing as we veer into a shadowed alley. The engine cuts off, plunging us into silence broken only by our ragged breathing. Without thinking, I'm moving across the leather seat, dress catching on the gearshift as I straddle her, the heat between us igniting like gasoline thrown on flames.

"Kira, we need to…"

"I need you," I interrupt, grinding down against her. "Right now. After what we just survived, I need to feel alive."

Her hands find my hips, steadying me. Our eyes lock, and the tension that's been building since the garden explodes.

I kiss her desperately, hands fumbling with her belt. Her fingers slide beneath my torn dress, finding me wet and wanting.

"Yes," I gasp as she enters me, two fingers curling inside. "Just like that."

The car rocks with our movements. I ride her hand, head thrown back, the streetlight painting my skin in shades of amber. She watches me, mesmerized, and I can see it in her eyes. She's chosen me. She's crossed the line.

When I come, it's with a broken cry, my body convulsing, nails digging into her shoulders.

We stay like that for a long moment, foreheads pressed together, hearts racing.

And I know…we both know…there's no going back.

Good. I never wanted to go back, anyway.

# CHAPTER FIVE

# Nadia

## THE WAREHOUSE

The Khlebnikov bread factory closed in 1997, a victim of post-Soviet economic collapse. Now it sits on the edge of the Pechatniki district, a monument to failed industry. The locals avoid it, say it's haunted by the workers who died when the roof collapsed in '95.

I don't believe in ghosts. But I believe in places that hold memory.

The factory is perfect. Isolated and forgotten, with enough structural integrity to be safe but decrepit enough that no one bothers to patrol it.

Tonight, it belongs to me and Kira.

I brought her here after the escape from the Volkov estate. We came through the broken fence and past the graffiti-covered walls.

It's one of my safe houses, a place Viktor doesn't know about, a place I keep for emergencies. The kind of place where you can make someone disappear if you need to.

I'm still not sure what I need.

The Mercedes sits outside, hidden behind a collapsed loading dock. Inside, moonlight streams through the broken roof in pale shafts, illuminating dust motes that dance like snow. The air smells of oil and decay, cold enough that our breath mists white.

Kira sits in a metal folding chair in the center of the space, hands zip-tied behind her back, ankles bound to the chair legs. Blood from the gala has dried on her torn dress, dark stains that look black in the dim light. Her hair is wild, makeup smudged, but her eyes are bright and alert.

Watching.

I circle her slowly, boots echoing on concrete, a knife loose in my hand. I've changed out of the midnight blue silk into tactical black pants, tank top, jacket. Back in my element. Back in control.

Except I'm not in control. Not really. Not what happened in the car. Not when she looks at me like that.

"Are we going to do this all night?" Kira asks, her voice cutting through the silence. "The silent treatment? The intimidation? It's very dramatic, but I'm getting bored."

I stop behind her, close enough to smell her perfume beneath the copper scent of blood. "You should be afraid."

"Should I?" She tilts her head back, trying to see my face. "You've had a dozen chances to kill me. You haven't. So either you're losing your touch, or you want something else."

"I want answers." I move around to face her, crouching down so we're eye level. "You knew I was coming for you from the beginning. You've been playing games, leaving notes, manipulating me. Why?"

Her smile is slow, dangerous. "Because you're the first interesting thing that's happened to me in years."

"That's not an answer."

"It's the only answer that matters." She leans forward as far as the restraints allow, her voice dropping to something intimate. "You're not here to kill me, Nadia. You're here because you want to understand me. Because I see you, and it terrifies you."

My jaw tightens. I stand abruptly, putting distance between us. "You don't know anything about me."

"Don't I? We're back to this?" Her eyes track my movement. "Orphaned young. Raised by the system. Viktor found you when you were…what, sixteen? Seventeen? He saw potential. He made you into his perfect weapon. Cold. Efficient. Empty."

Each word lands like a blow. I force my expression to remain neutral.

"But you're not empty," she continues, relentless. "That's the lie you tell yourself. That's the mask you wear. I've seen your work, Nadia. The black dahlias. The ritual. You think murder can be art, that if you make it beautiful enough, it means something."

"Shut up."

"You want to be seen," she says, refusing to stop. "You want someone to look at you and understand that you're not just a killer. That you're more than what Viktor made you."

I cross the space in three strides, grab her chin, force her to meet my eyes. "I said shut up."

She smiles, fearless. "Make me."

For a long moment, we stare at each other. My hand is shaking, with rage or something else, I can't tell. Her pulse beats visibly in her throat, rapid but steady.

Her voice is soft now, almost tender. "You're the only person who's ever looked at me and seen something other than a broken toy or a liability. You see the monster, Nadia. And you don't flinch."

I release her, step back. My mind is racing, trying to regain the control I lost somewhere between the gala and this moment. I'm supposed to be interrogating her, figuring out her angle, deciding whether to eliminate her or use her.

Instead, I feel like I'm the one being dissected.

"What do you want from me?" I ask.

"Everything." Her answer is immediate, honest. "I want you to stop pretending you're dead inside. I want you to feel something real. I want..." She pauses, something vulnerable flickering across her face. "I want not to be alone."

The confession hangs in the air between us.

I walk to the broken window, look out at the city lights in the distance. Behind me, I hear her shift in the chair, the plastic zip-ties creaking.

"I've been alone my whole life," I say, not turning around. "Even when I'm in a room full of people. Even when I'm standing over a body. Especially then."

"I know," she says softly.

"Viktor trained me to be a ghost. To move through the world without leaving a trace, without forming attachments. He said emotions were a weakness. That caring about anything would get me killed."

"And you believed him."

"I had to." My hands clench on the windowsill. "Because the alternative was..." My voice catches. "The alternative was admitting that I'm human. That I want things. That I'm capable of..."

"Love?" she finishes.

I turn to face her. "Don't."

"Why not? It's what this is, isn't it?" Her eyes are bright, fierce. "You feel it too. This pull. This recognition. We're the same, you and I. We're both monsters pretending to be human. Or humans pretending to be monsters. I'm not sure which anymore."

"We're not the same."

"Aren't we?" She leans forward. "You kill for Viktor. I kill for myself. But we both kill. We both understand that violence can be beautiful, that destruction is sometimes the only honest thing in a world of lies."

I cross back to her, kneel in front of the chair. I pull out my knife, and for a moment, her breath hitches. But I just cut the zip-ties on her wrists, then her ankles.

She rubs her wrists, watching me warily. "What are you doing?"

"I don't know." I sit back on my heels, the knife still in my hand. "I should kill you. Viktor expects a body. The Sokolovs want you dead. The Volkovs want you dead. Everyone wants you dead."

"And you?" she asks. "What do you want?"

I look at her, really look at her. Wild hair, fierce eyes, blood on her dress and defiance in every line of her body. She's chaos and beauty and danger, everything I've been trained to eliminate.

Everything I want.

"I want to see what happens," I admit.

Her smile could light the room on fire. "Finally. An honest answer."

She stands slowly, and I rise with her. We're close now, close enough that I can see the faint scar on her lower lip, the way her pupils dilate.

"So what now?" she asks.

I should have an answer. Should have a plan. But standing here, in this abandoned warehouse with moonlight streaming through broken windows and a woman who sees through all my carefully constructed walls, I have nothing.

Except want.

"Now," I say, my voice rough, "we see if you're right. About us being the same."

She reaches up, her fingers tracing the line of my jaw. "And if I am?"

"Then we'll burn the world down together."

Her laugh is breathless, delighted. "Promise?"

Instead of answering, I grab the front of her dress and pull her into a kiss.

It isn't gentle. It's hunger and desperation and months of

denial crashing together. Her hands fist in my hair, pulling me closer, and my knife clatters to the floor, forgotten.

We stumble backward, her back hitting the wall, and I press against her, one hand braced beside her head, the other at her waist. She bites my lower lip hard enough to draw blood, and I gasp, pulling back just enough to look at her.

Her eyes are wild, pupils blown, lips swollen. "Still think we're not the same?"

I kiss her again, tasting copper and champagne and something darker. My hands find the zipper of her torn dress, dragging it down slowly, deliberately. The fabric pools at her feet, revealing pale skin marked with old scars and fresh bruises.

"Beautiful," I whisper, tracing the line of her collarbone with my lips.

Her breath hitches. Her fingers work at the buttons of my shirt, impatient, tearing one loose in her haste. "I want to feel you. All of you."

We sink to the floor together, my jacket spread beneath us. My mouth travels down her throat, her sternum, the soft curve of her breast. She arches into my touch, fingers digging into my shoulders hard enough to leave marks.

Her voice breaks on a single word: "Please." The sound of it, raw, desperate, it sends a shiver through me.

My hand slides between her thighs, finding her wet and wanting. Her hips buck against my palm, seeking friction, seeking release. I watch her face as I work my fingers inside, mesmerized by the way her eyes roll back, the way her mouth falls open in a silent cry.

"Look at me," I command, and her eyes snap to mine, green and desperate and utterly surrendered.

The cold concrete beneath us, the broken city around us. None of it matters. There's only this: her trembling beneath me, coming apart with my name on her lips.

Afterwards, we lie tangled together, skin slick with sweat, hearts still racing. Her head rests on my bare chest, listening to my heartbeat. The warehouse is silent except for our breathing and the distant sound of sirens.

"What happens now?" she asks quietly.

I run my fingers through her hair, still trying to process what we've done. What I've done. I've crossed a line I can't uncross, made a choice that will have consequences I can't predict.

"I don't know," I admit. "Viktor will expect a report. When I don't give him one, when I don't deliver your body, he'll send someone else."

"Then we kill them."

"And then?"

"And then we keep killing them." She props herself up on one elbow, looking down at me. "Until there's no one left to send. Until we're free."

"That's not a plan. That's suicide."

"Maybe." She traces a finger along the scar on my collarbone. "But at least it's ours. At least we chose it."

I catch her hand, hold it against my chest where my heart is still racing. "I've never chosen anything before. Viktor chose for me. The world chose for me. I just... existed."

"Then choose this." Her voice is fierce, urgent. "Choose me. Choose us. Choose to burn it all down and see what grows in the ashes."

I look up at her. This wild, broken, beautiful woman has torn through my life like a hurricane, leaving nothing standing. I think about Viktor's disappointed face when he learns of my betrayal. About the Sokolovs and the Volkovs and all the people who will come for us. About the blood that will be spilled, the bridges that will burn.

And I think about the alternative: walking away, completing the mission, going back to being Viktor's perfect weapon. Cold. Empty. Alone.

I meet her eyes. "Yes."

"Yes?" Her voice catches.

"Yes." I pull her down, my lips finding hers, sealing our fate. "We'll watch it all burn."

She breaks the kiss, her breath warm against my cheek. "You realize we're signing our death warrants."

"Would you rather live forever as someone else's weapon?"

We hold each other as dawn breaks through the windows, painting the warehouse in shades of gold and amber. Outside, the city wakes, unaware that two of its most dangerous women have just declared war on everything.

I feel something unfamiliar stirring in my chest, something that might be hope or might be terror. Probably both.

For the first time in fifteen years, I feel alive.

And for the first time in my life, I'm not alone.

# KIRA

## HOURS LATER...

I wake up wrapped in Nadia's jacket, her body warm against mine, and for a moment I forget where I am. Then I remember, the warehouse, the escape, the way she looked at me when she cut the zip-ties.

The way she kissed me like she was drowning and I was air.

I shift slightly, not wanting to wake her, and study her face in the early morning light. She looks younger when she sleeps, the hard edges softened, the walls temporarily down. There's a vulnerability there that she'd never show while awake.

God, I'm in trouble.

I've spent my whole life burning through people, relationships, connections. Everything I touch turns to ash, eventually. It's safer that way. Can't lose what you never really had.

But this...her. It's different. She sees me. Really sees me. Not the crazy daughter or the family embarrassment or the broken thing that needs fixing. She sees all my jagged edges, and instead of cutting herself on them, she kissed me.

She chose me.

And now we're both fucked.

"Any regrets?" My voice catches, betraying me.

The silence stretches between us. I count her breaths, one, two, three, each one a lifetime. My ribs constrict around my lungs, bracing for the inevitable: *This was a mistake. I can't betray Viktor. I'm leaving.*

Instead, she brushes her lips against my forehead, her breath warm against my skin. She meets my eyes, unflinching. "No."

Something wild and dangerous unfurls in my chest. "Ready to set the world on fire?"

"The world can wait." She sits up, scanning the warehouse with predator's eyes. "Viktor won't. We need to move."

Even naked and vulnerable, she's calculating sight lines and exit strategies. My heart stutters. Fuck.

"I've got a place," I say, watching her collect scattered clothing with military efficiency. "Off-books. Not even in my family's records."

She nods once, sharp, already transforming back into the weapon they made her. I watch her check the magazine in her gun, the fluid economy of her movements hypnotic.

"Nadia." Her name stops her cold. "Thank you for choosing me instead of killing me."

A muscle jumps in her jaw. "Don't thank me yet. We've painted targets on our backs."

I pull on my ruined dress, feeling oddly powerful in its tatters. "At least we're in the crosshairs together."

Something almost like a smile ghosts across her lips. "Together," she echoes, testing the word like an unfamiliar weapon.

We slip out as dawn bleeds across the sky, leaving nothing behind but phantom impressions on dust-covered floors.

Ahead lies a gauntlet of killers, syndicate soldiers, and impossible odds.

For the first time since they locked me in that psychiatric ward, I'm not afraid of what comes next.

Two days later, we face our first test as partners, not running, not surviving, but hunting.

# CHAPTER SIX

# NADIA

## THE FIRST JOINT KILL

The hotel is the kind of place that asks no questions. Peeling wallpaper, a flickering neon sign from the pawnshop across the street, casting red and blue shadows through thin curtains. The carpet smells of cigarettes and desperation, and the floorboards beneath it groan when Kira sits on the edge of the bed, crossing her legs with deliberate slowness.

"He'll be here in ten minutes," she says, checking her phone. Her voice is light, almost playful, but I can see the tension in her shoulders, the way her fingers drum against her thigh.

I stand by the window, watching the street below. A few drunks stumble past, a car with a broken muffler rattles by. Normal city sounds. The world going about its business, unaware that death is being prepared three floors up.

"You're nervous," I observe.

Her laugh is sharp. "Excited. There's a difference."

"Is there?"

"For me, yes." She stands and smooths down her dress. Red and tight, the kind that makes men stupid. "This is different from watching you work. This time, we do it together."

Together. The word still feels foreign, dangerous. I've worked alone for fifteen years. Solo jobs meant solo control, solo survival. But here I am with a woman who makes my pulse race and my carefully constructed walls crumble, about to commit murder as a duet.

"Tell me again," I say. "Everything you know about him."

She moves to stand beside me at the window, our shoulders almost touching. "Yuri Federov. The Sokolov syndicate's accountant. Forty-three years old, married, two kids. He's been skimming for months. Small amounts, but enough to notice if you're looking. They want him dealt with quietly."

"And you volunteered us."

"I volunteered me. You came along for the ride." Her smile is wicked. "Though I'm not complaining about the company."

I turn to face her. In the dim light, she looks almost ethereal. Pale skin, dark lips, eyes that hold both madness and something softer. Something that makes my chest ache.

"This isn't a game," I say quietly.

"Everything's a game." She reaches up, traces the line of my jaw with one finger. "The question is whether you're playing with me or against me."

Before I can answer, a knock at the door. Three quick raps, then two slow ones. The signal.

Her expression shifts instantly, the wildness giving way to something calculated, predatory. She moves to the door, hips swaying, and I melt into the shadows beside the bathroom.

When she opens the door, Yuri Federov stands in the hallway, nervous sweat already beading on his forehead. He's exactly as his file described…average height, thinning hair, soft around the middle. The kind of man who thought he was cleverer than he actually was.

"You're alone?" he asks, peering past her into the room.

"Of course." Her voice is honey and poison. "Did you bring what I asked for?"

He holds up a briefcase. "The files. Everything you wanted. But I need guarantees…"

"Come inside first." She steps back, letting him enter. "We can discuss guarantees once I've verified the information."

Yuri hesitates, but greed wins over caution. It always does. He steps into the room, and she closes the door behind him with a soft click.

"Put the briefcase on the bed," she instructs, moving to pour two glasses of vodka from a bottle on the nightstand. "We should toast our new partnership."

Yuri sets down the briefcase, his eyes darting around the room. Looking for threats, for cameras, for anything that might indicate this is a trap. But I'm a ghost, invisible in my stillness.

"I don't know about this," Yuri says. "If your father finds out…"

"My father won't find out." She hands him a glass, raises her own. "To secrets."

He drinks. She doesn't.

As Yuri lowers his glass, I move. Three silent steps, and I'm behind him, one arm around his throat, the other hand pressing a cloth soaked in chloroform over his nose and mouth.

He struggles, tries to scream, but my grip is iron. Kira watches, her eyes bright with something between fascination and arousal, as Yuri's movements grow weaker, slower, until finally he goes limp.

I lower him to the floor, check his pulse. Still alive. For now.

"Tie him to the chair," I say.

We work in silence, efficient. She drags the desk chair to the center of the room while I retrieve zip-ties from my bag. Within minutes, Yuri is secured, head lolling forward, unconscious.

I stand back, studying our work. Professional. Clean. Exactly as it should be.

She circles the chair slowly, trailing her fingers along Yuri's shoulders. "How long until he wakes up?"

"Five minutes. Maybe ten."

"Good." She pulls a knife from her purse. Small, wickedly sharp, the handle inlaid with mother-of-pearl. "I want to see his eyes when he realizes."

I feel something cold settle in my stomach. I've killed dozens of people, but always quickly, efficiently. There's a difference between execution and torture, between necessity and cruelty.

"Kira..."

"Don't." She turns to face me, and the wildness is back in her eyes. "Don't tell me to be gentle. Don't tell me to make it quick. He stole from the family. He put his wife and children at risk for money. He deserves to suffer."

"It's not about what he deserves. It's about..."

"Control?" She steps closer, the knife still in her hand. "Is that what you're afraid of? That I'll lose control? That I'll enjoy it too much?"

I hold my ground. "Yes."

Her laugh is breathless. "Then you don't know me at all, Angel. I always lose control. That's the point."

She turns back to Yuri just as he begins to stir, groaning, his head lifting slowly.

"Welcome back," she says sweetly.

Yuri's eyes snap open. It takes him a moment to process. The chair, the restraints, Kira standing before him with a knife. Then panic sets in.

"What...what is this? Kira, please, I brought the files, I did everything you asked..."

"I know." She crouches down, bringing herself eye-level with him. "And I'm grateful. Really. But you see, there's a problem. You stole. And theft, well...that requires conse-quences."

"I'll pay it back! Every ruble, I swear..."

"Shhh." She presses a finger to his lips. "It's too late for that."

She stands, looks over at me. "Do you want to start, or should I?"

This is the moment. The choice. I could walk away, refuse to participate in whatever she has planned. I could maintain my professional distance, my carefully constructed moral lines.

But when I look at her. Wild, beautiful, terrifying. I realize those lines have already been crossed. The moment I chose not to kill her, the moment I kissed her in the warehouse, the moment I decided to burn the world down with her. All of it led here.

To this room. To this choice. To this woman who sees through every mask I wear and loves the monster underneath.

"We do it together," I say.

Her smile is incandescent, dangerous.

The interrogation is brief but thorough. I extract what we need about the Sokolov finances and their vulnerabilities. Kira watches, learning.

When there's nothing left to learn, I hand her the garrote wire.

"Are you sure?" I ask.

"I need to do this," she says. "I need to know I can."

I understand. This isn't about cruelty. It's about power. About reclaiming hers.

She moves behind the chair. Her hands shake as she positions the wire. Then she pulls.

It takes longer than it should, but she doesn't let go. When it's over, she turns to me, tears streaming, and laughs.

"I don't feel guilty," she breathes, searching my eyes. "Should I?"

"I stopped feeling guilty years ago."

"Then we really are the same." Her smile is radiant and terrible. "Monsters pretending to be human."

I reach into my bag and withdraw a black dahlia. I tuck it into Yuri's shirt pocket, our signature, our calling card.

Then I take her hand and lead her to the bathroom.

We clean up in silence, washing blood from our hands, our clothes. I'm methodical, checking for evidence, making sure nothing can trace back to us. She watches me work, still trembling slightly, still riding the high of what we've done.

"What now?" she asks as I pull out a disposable phone to make the call. Anonymous tip to the police, ensuring the body will be found but not too quickly.

"Now we leave. Separately. You go first, take the back stairs. I'll wipe down the room and follow in ten minutes."

"And then?"

I look at her. "Then we meet at the safe house. The one you think I don't know about."

Her eyebrows rise. "You've been tracking me?"

"Since the beginning."

"Good." She moves closer, presses her forehead against mine. "I'd be disappointed if you hadn't."

We stand like that for a moment, breathing the same air, two killers finding strange comfort in each other's darkness.

"Nadia," she whispers. "Thank you. For not stopping me. For letting me be… this."

"I couldn't stop you if I tried."

"You could. But you didn't." She kisses me once more, soft and brief. "That's why I love you."

The words hang in the air between us, heavy and dangerous and true.

I don't say them back. Can't. Not yet. But I cup her face in my hands and kiss her hard enough to bruise, and that's answer enough.

When we finally pull apart, she grabs her purse and heads for the door. She pauses in the doorway, looks back over her shoulder.

"Don't take too long," she says. "I'll be waiting."

Then she's gone, and I'm alone with the body and the blood and the terrifying realization that I've just crossed a line I can never uncross.

I've killed before. But never like this. Never as an act of devotion.

Never for love.

# KIRA

I make it three blocks before I have to stop, lean against a wall, and try to remember how to breathe.

I actually killed him.

My hands are still shaking, adrenaline and shock warring in my system. I can still feel the wire in my hands, still hear the sounds he made, still see the moment when the light left his eyes.

And the worst part? The part that should terrify me?

I feel alive.

Not guilty. Not horrified. Not broken by what I've done.

Alive.

I laugh, the sound echoing off the empty street, and a few late-night stragglers give me a wide berth. Good. Let them think I'm crazy. Let them see the monster.

Nadia saw the monster and didn't run. She handed me the wire and let me become exactly what I needed to be.

That's why I love you.

The words slipped out before I could stop them. Too soon. Too dangerous. Too real. But I meant them. God help me, I meant every syllable.

I push off the wall and keep walking, heading toward my safe house. The apartment I rented under a false name, paid for with money I skimmed from my family years ago. My escape route. My sanctuary.

Now it's ours.

My phone buzzes. A text from an unknown number, but I know it's her.

Clear. On my way.

I smile, tucking the phone away, and pick up my pace. By the time I reach the apartment, I've almost stopped shaking.

Almost.

I let myself in, lock the door behind me, and immediately strip off my dress. I stand in the shower, watching remnants of pink water swirl down the drain, and replay the whole night in my head.

The way Nadia moved. Efficient, deadly, beautiful. The way she looked at me when I asked to do it myself. The way she held me after.

We're bound now. Blood and flowers. Death and devotion.

When I get out of the shower, I hear the door open. Close. Lock.

"Kira?" Her voice, cautious.

"Bedroom," I call back.

She appears in the doorway, still in her tactical black, and for a moment we just look at each other. Two killers. Two ghosts. Two halves of something dark and consuming.

Then she crosses the room and pulls me into her arms, and I realize I'm crying.

"I know," she whispers, holding me as I shake. "I know."

We don't talk about it. Don't analyze or justify or rationalize. We just hold each other in the darkness, two monsters finding strange comfort in shared monstrosity.

Eventually, she pulls back, cups my face in her hands.

"What you said before," she starts. "About love…"

"Forget it," I interrupt, suddenly terrified of what she might say. "It was the adrenaline talking. I didn't mean…"

"I feel the same," she says.

The world stops.

"What?"

"I feel it too." Her gray eyes are serious, vulnerable in a way I've never seen. "I don't know when it happened. Maybe the warehouse. Maybe the moment you smiled at me in your father's garden. Maybe the second I saw your photograph and felt something other than emptiness for the first time in fifteen years."

She kisses me softly. "You're everything to me, Kira Sokolov. And it terrifies me."

I laugh through my tears, pulling her closer. "Good. We should both be terrified."

"Why?"

"Because love makes us vulnerable. And vulnerable people don't survive in our world."

"Then we'll have to change our world," she says, and kisses me again.

We make love slowly this time, tenderly, washing away the blood and the violence with something softer. And when we finally fall asleep, tangled together in my bed, I feel something I haven't felt since I was a child.

Safe.

It won't last, a voice whispers in my head. Nothing good ever does.

But for now, wrapped in her arms, I let myself believe in impossible things.

In love. In safety. In us.

# CHAPTER SEVEN
## KIRA

### JEALOUSY'S EDGE

The nightclub is called Inferno, and it lives up to its name. Red lights pulse in time with the bass, casting everything in shades of blood and shadow. Bodies move on the dance floor like a single organism, writhing, grinding, lost in the music and the heat and the chemical haze that hangs in the air.

I'm at the bar, laughing at something the bartender said, my hand resting casually on a blonde woman's arm. She's beautiful. Model beautiful, with sharp cheekbones and legs that go on forever. Her name is Svetlana, and she's been flirting with me for the past twenty minutes.

I'm not interested.

But Nadia is watching from across the room, and I want to see what she'll do.

This is a terrible idea, the rational part of my brain observes.

I know, the rest of me thinks back. That's why I'm doing it.

Svetlana leans in, whispers something in my ear about going somewhere quieter, and I smile that smile, the one that promises danger and pleasure in equal measure. Out of the corner of my eye, I see Nadia set down her glass and stand.

There we go.

"Another time," I tell Svetlana, and turn away, leaving her standing there confused.

I can feel Nadia approaching, that electric awareness I always have when she's near. Then her hand is on the small of my back, possessive and warm.

"Having fun?" she asks, her voice low and dangerous.

I turn, grinning. "Nadia! I was just telling Svetlana here about the art exhibit we saw last week. You remember, the one with all the violence and flowers?"

Svetlana smiles, oblivious to the tension. "It sounds fascinating. I'd love to see it."

"It's closed now," Nadia says flatly. "Permanently."

"Oh, that's too bad." Svetlana's hand is still on my arm. "Maybe the three of us could get drinks sometime? I know this great place in…"

"No." Nadia's voice is ice.

Svetlana blinks, finally sensing the danger. "I… I should go. Nice meeting you, Kira."

She disappears into the crowd, and I turn to face Nadia fully, barely containing my delight.

"Jealous, Angel?"

"No." The lie is obvious.

"Liar." I press closer, my body warm against hers. "Your eyes get darker when you're jealous. Did you know that? Like storm clouds."

"I don't get jealous."

"You're adorable when you lie." My hand slides up her chest, fingers playing with the collar of her shirt. "What were you going to do if I'd left with her? Follow us? Watch? Join in?"

She grabs my wrist, holds it firm. "I was going to kill her."

The words send a thrill through me. "Really?"

"Really."

"Show me."

Her grip tightens. "What?"

"Show me." My voice is urgent now, hungry. "Prove it. Prove you'd kill for me."

# NADIA

This is insane. We're in a crowded nightclub, surrounded by witnesses, with security cameras everywhere. This is the opposite of everything I've been trained to do.

But when I look into Kira's eyes, wild and desperate and absolutely serious. I feel something shift inside my chest. Something that's been locked away for fifteen years, something I thought was dead.

Possessiveness. Devotion. Love twisted into something dark and dangerous.

"Not here," I say. "But I'll show you."

Her smile is incandescent. "Promise?"

"Promise."

We leave the club an hour later. I've been watching Svetlana all night, memorizing her patterns, her friends, the way she checks her phone every ten minutes. When she finally leaves, stumbling slightly from too many drinks, Kira and I follow at a distance.

The streets are quieter here, away from the club district. Residential buildings with darkened windows, a few late-night convenience stores, the occasional taxi passing by.

Svetlana is texting someone, not paying attention to her surroundings. Easy prey.

I move like smoke, closing the distance in seconds. One hand over her mouth, the other arm around her waist, dragging her into an alley before she can scream.

Kira follows, her heels clicking on the pavement, unhurried.

In the alley, I press Svetlana against the wall, keep my hand firmly over her mouth. Her eyes are wide with terror, mascara already running as tears stream down her face.

"Shhh," I whisper. "This isn't personal."

It's a lie. It's entirely personal.

Kira appears beside us, studying Svetlana with clinical interest. "She really is beautiful. I can see why you're threatened."

"I'm not threatened."

"Then why are we here?" She tilts her head. "Why are you about to kill a woman whose only crime was flirting with me?"

"Because you're mine." The words come out fierce, possessive. "Because I don't share."

Her smile is radiant. "Say it again."

"You're mine."

"Again."

"Mine." My hand moves to Svetlana's throat, applying just enough pressure to make my point. "Only mine."

"God, I love you," Kira breathes.

She kisses me then, hard and desperate, while Svetlana struggles weakly between us. When we break apart, Kira pulls a knife from her purse, the same mother-of-pearl handled blade from the hotel room.

"Let me," she says. "I want to do this for you."

I hesitate. This is different from Yuri. Yuri had been a job, a target, someone who'd committed crimes that warranted death in our world. Svetlana is innocent. Her only mistake was being in the wrong place at the wrong time, catching the attention of the wrong woman.

"Kira…"

"Please." Her eyes are pleading. "Let me prove I'd kill for you too."

And that's the moment I realize how far we've fallen. How completely we've lost ourselves in each other. How the line between love and madness has blurred until it doesn't exist anymore.

I think of my brother Alexei. How I killed to protect him, how it wasn't enough, how he died anyway. I think of every person I've loved being torn away, how loving me is a death sentence. And now here's Kira, asking to cross the same line, to become the same kind of monster. Not because she has to, but because she wants to prove we're the same.

This isn't just murder. This is Kira claiming me, marking our bond in blood. This is possession so complete it demands sacrifice. An innocent life offered up not to necessity, but to us. To what we've become together.

I should stop this. Should walk away. Should remember that there are rules, codes, lines that shouldn't be crossed even by people like us. But I've spent fifteen years alone, and Kira is the first person who's ever made me feel like I exist beyond my function as a weapon.

And if this is what it costs to keep her. If this is the price of not being alone, then I'll pay it. We'll pay it together.

God help us both.

Instead, I step aside.

# KIRA

I move in front of Svetlana, knife in hand. She's beautiful, terrified, innocent. Everything I'm not.

And she touched what's mine.

"I'm sorry," I say, and I mean it. "But you touched something that belongs to me."

The knife is quick, efficient. I learned from watching Nadia, where to cut, how deep, how to make it fast. Svetlana's struggles weaken, then stop. Her body slumps, and I catch her, lower her gently to the ground.

For a moment, we both stand there, breathing hard, staring at what I've done.

Then I turn to Nadia, blood on my hands and tears in my eyes. "Are you happy now? Is this what you wanted?"

She pulls me close, kisses my forehead, my cheeks, my lips. Her mouth tastes like copper and devotion.

"What have we become?" she whispers against my skin.

"Something beautiful," I answer, and feel her shudder.

"Something terrible," she corrects, fingers digging into my hips.

I laugh, the sound broken and wild. "Isn't that the same thing?"

She pulls out a black dahlia; she always carries one now, just in case and places it on Svetlana's chest. Our signature. Our promise. Our curse.

Then she takes my hand, and we walk out of the alley into the night, leaving death and flowers in our wake.

# NADIA

I don't take us back to Kira's safe house. Instead, I lead us to one of my own places. A small apartment in a building that doesn't ask questions, with windows that overlook the river.

Inside, I turn on the shower, strip off my bloodstained clothes, and pull her in with me.

The water runs hot, steam filling the small bathroom. I press her against the tile wall, water streaming over both our bodies, washing away blood and violence.

Her legs wrap around my waist, pulling me closer. "I need you," she whispers against my ear. "I need to feel something other than this."

My fingers find her center, circling slowly, teasingly. She whimpers, grinding against my hand, chasing the pleasure that will drown out everything else.

"That's it," I murmur, my free hand tangling in her wet hair. "Let go. I've got you."

She comes with a broken sob, her body shaking, tears mixing with the shower spray. I hold her through it, whispering reassurances in Russian, words of love and devotion that I never dared speak before.

When her breathing steadies, she slides down to her knees, looking up at me with eyes still bright with tears. "My turn."

Her mouth is hot and eager, her tongue skilled. My head falls back against the tile, one hand bracing myself, the other buried in her hair. The sensation is overwhelming, pleasure edged with the ghost of violence, tenderness born from brutality.

AFTERWARD, WRAPPED IN TOWELS AND SITTING ON THE bathroom floor, she traces the dahlia scar on my thigh.

"We're bound now," she says. "Blood and flowers. Death and devotion."

"Yes."

"There's no going back."

She looks up at me, green eyes serious. "Do you regret it?"

I think about Svetlana, about the life we took for no reason except jealousy and possession. I think about all the lines I've crossed, all the rules I've broken, all the parts of myself I've lost in the pursuit of this dark, consuming love.

"No," I say, and mean it. "I don't regret you."

She smiles, presses her forehead against mine. "Good. Because I'm not done with you yet."

"What do you mean?"

"I mean..." She pulls back, and there's something wild in her eyes again, something manic and beautiful and terrifying. "I mean, we're just getting started. The Sokolovs, the Volkovs, Viktor, all of them. They think they can control us, use us, own us. But they're wrong."

"Kira..."

"We're going to burn it all down, Nadia. Every family, every syndicate, every person who ever tried to make us into something we're not."

"You're talking about war."

"I'm talking about freedom." Her fingers trace my collarbone. "I'm talking about writing our names in their blood."

"And after?"

"After we'll disappear. Just you and me, somewhere they can never find us."

It's insane. It's impossible. It's a suicide mission dressed up as a love story.

And I find myself nodding.

"Okay," I say. "Let's burn it all down." I reach for her hand, intertwining our fingers, feeling her pulse against mine, two hearts beating in perfect, violent synchrony. The rhythm of destruction. The cadence of revenge.

# KIRA

Her laugh echoes through the small bathroom, wild and free and utterly unhinged. I pull her into another kiss, and she tastes like promises and the end of everything.

Outside, the city continues its endless dance of light and shadow, unaware that two of its most dangerous inhabitants have just declared war on the world.

And in the morning, when the police find Svetlana's body in the alley with a black dahlia on her chest, the city will begin to understand that The Black Dahlia and the Thorn Queen are no longer playing by anyone's rules but their own.

We're bound by blood and flowers, by jealousy and devotion, by a love so dark and consuming that it can only end one way.

In fire.

In death.

In legend.

But tonight, wrapped in her arms, I let myself believe in impossible things.

In us. In always. In together.
Even if together means burning the world to ashes.

# CHAPTER EIGHT
# NADIA

## TWIN BOMBINGS

### LOCATION ONE: THE POLICE STATION

The police station is a fortress of concrete and fluorescent lights. Detective Markovic sits at her desk at 3 AM, surrounded by case files, hunting the Black Dahlia.

She doesn't know that in seven minutes, her world will explode.

I move through the basement corridors in a stolen uniform, passing checkpoints without question. The evidence room is a maze of shelves and boxes. I find what I need, evidence from the Sokolov and Volkov investigations.

I place the device and set the timer. Five minutes.

As I leave, I pass Markovic in the hallway. Our eyes meet for half a second.

"Working late?" she asks.

"Always," I reply, and keep walking.

Outside, I check my phone. Kira's in position at the Volkov mansion. We're really doing this.

I think about the people inside. Cops doing their jobs. Clerks. Janitors.

Collateral damage, Viktor's voice echoes. But this isn't Viktor's mission. This is mine. Ours.

I drive to the rendezvous point. A rooftop where I'll have a clear view of both explosions.

If she makes it out.

I check my watch. Three minutes.

# KIRA

## LOCATION TWO: VOLKOV MANSION GARAGE

The Volkov mansion garage is massive, filled with luxury vehicles that cost more than most people make in a lifetime. Each one is a symbol of everything I was born into and rejected. Each one represents blood money, stolen lives, the price of power.

Time to make them pay.

I crouch beneath a black Mercedes, my hands steady despite the adrenaline singing through my veins. The explosives are elegant in their simplicity. Enough to take out the garage and the wing of the mansion above it, but not so much that it would kill indiscriminately.

I have my targets, the Volkov brothers who tried to use me as a pawn, the lieutenants who ordered the hit at the gala. The ones who deserve this.

I think about Nadia, across the city, planting her own bomb. We synchronized our watches, planned every detail. Two strikes at once. The police who hunt us, the criminals who want us dead.

Burn it all down, she said. Leave nothing but ashes.

God, I love her.

The thought doesn't scare me anymore. It should. Love is dangerous, love is weakness, love gets you killed. But with Nadia, it feels like the only honest thing in my life.

I set the timer and crawl out from under the car. My dress: red silk. Because I believe in making a statement, it's streaked with grease and dirt. I don't care.

As I move through the mansion's service corridors, I pass a young maid carrying fresh linens. The girl can't be more than sixteen, eyes wide with the terror of working for monsters.

I stop her, press a wad of cash into her hands.

"Get out," I whisper. "Run. Don't come back."

She stares at me, confused.

"Now," I say, my voice sharp.

The maid runs.

At least I saved one.

I check my watch. Two minutes.

Time to go.

# NADIA

## THE CONVERGENCE

I stand on the rooftop, watching both locations through binoculars. The police station to my left, the Volkov mansion to my right. The city spread between them, unaware of what's coming.

My phone is in my hand, Kira's number ready to dial if something goes wrong. If she needs extraction. If...

Don't think about it. She'll make it.

Thirty seconds.

I count them down in my head, the way I've counted down before. But this time it's different. This time, I'm not just killing targets. I'm destroying evidence, eliminating threats, declaring war on everyone who ever tried to control us.

This time, I'm choosing chaos.

Ten seconds.

I think about Viktor's face when he finds out. About the

disappointment, the rage, the certainty that he'll send everyone he has to hunt us down.

Let him come. We'll be ready.

Five seconds.

I see movement at the Volkov mansion, a figure in red, running across the lawn. Kira. She made it out.

Relief floods through me so intensely it's almost painful.

Zero.

The police station bomb detonates first.

The evidence room erupts in a ball of fire and smoke, the blast tearing through two floors, bringing down part of the building's west wing. Even from here, I can hear the alarms shrieking, people screaming. I watch through the binoculars as Detective Markovic is thrown from her chair by the shock-wave, blood running down her face as she crawls through the chaos.

I did that. I destroyed lives, ended careers, and maybe killed people who didn't deserve it.

The thought should bother me more than it does.

Thirty seconds later, the Volkov mansion garage explodes.

The blast is massive, a column of fire that lights up the night sky. The garage collapses, taking with it half a dozen cars and the mansion's entire east wing. The Volkov brothers, meeting in the study directly above, don't have time to scream.

I lower the binoculars and allow myself a small smile.

We did that.

My phone buzzes. A text from Kira:

See you on the other side, Angel.

I type back:

Already here. Waiting.

# KIRA

I burst onto the rooftop, lungs burning, adrenaline crackling in my veins. Below, the city's an inferno: twin pillars of smoke clawing at the night sky, sirens weaving a frantic chorus through the streets. Embers drift upward like malevolent fireflies.

And there she is, Nadia, my angel of destruction, poised at the parapet's edge. Her silhouette is carved in flame, those gray eyes cold as ice, drinking in the ruins we've wrought.

I charge forward, heart hammering so loud I swear she can hear it. When she turns, her face is a frozen mask for a single heartbeat, then her lips curve into a fierce, triumphant smile. Pride. Relief. Maybe even love.

I throw myself into her arms, crash my lips against hers. Hard. "We did it. We actually fucking did it."

Her arms lock around me, and I feel her heart pound against mine. "There's no turning back now," she whispers.

I grin, every nerve alight. "Good. I never wanted to."

We cling together, witnesses to the city's collapse: burning towers, crumpled cars, silhouettes fleeing through smoke. But all I feel is Nadia's warmth, the sharp tang of smoke and lipstick on my tongue.

This, this is freedom.

A hush falls, broken only by distant cries. I tilt my head. "So? What now?"

She fishes a champagne bottle from her jacket, probably filched from one of the vaults. Pops the cork, takes a long pull, then hands it to me. "We celebrate," she declares.

I laugh, tilting the bottle to my lips, the bubbly liquid splashing against my chin. "You learn fast." "You learn fast."

She rolls her eyes. "You're a terrible influence."

"The best kind," I shoot back, raising my bottle.

We pass the champagne as emergency lights paint the city red and blue. Somewhere below, Marković hauls bodies from wreckage. Somewhere, syndicate bosses bark orders. Somewhere, Viktor is realizing his perfect weapon just turned on him.

Up here, though? We're untouchable.

"Dance with me," I say, surprising us both.

"There's no music," she counters.

"There's always music." I pull out my phone, scroll, hit play. A solitary violin concerto unfurls, dark, haunting, desperate.

I offer my hand. She lets me lead her into a slow spin at the rooftop's edge. Champagne tumbles forgotten, sparks from the fires below swirling around us. Her head settles on my shoulder, my arms cradle her waist. Two killers finding grace in each other's shadows.

When the final notes fade, we freeze, foreheads touching, breaths mingling.

"I love you," I whisper, voice trembling. "I love you so much it terrifies me."

She presses a soft kiss to my lips. "Good. You should be afraid. We're already at war."

"I know," I smile, fierce and free. "But at least we fight together."

"Together," she echoes, and we stand united against the burning world beneath us.

# NADIA

We stay on that rooftop until dawn, watching the fires burn down to embers, watching the city wake up to the devastation we caused. And when the sun finally rises, painting the sky in shades of pink and gold, we climb down and disappear into the streets.

The hunt is on. The city wants us dead. But we have each other and for now, that's everything.

As we walk through the early morning streets, Kira's hand

in mine, I realize something profound: I'm not Viktor's weapon anymore. I'm not the Black Dahlia, the ghost, the perfect killing machine.

I'm just Nadia. A woman who chose love over duty, chaos over control, life over the empty existence I'd been living.

And if that choice kills me, at least I'll die having felt something real.

"Where to?" Kira asks, squeezing my hand.

I think about the safe houses I've prepared, the escape routes I've memorized, the contingencies I've planned. But none of it matters anymore. We're not running. We're not hiding.

We're burning the world down, one target at a time.

"Wherever we want," I say. "We're free now."

She laughs, that bright, manic sound I've come to love. "Free to die spectacularly."

"The best kind of freedom."

We disappear into the city as the sirens wail behind us, two ghosts haunting each other, two monsters finding love in the darkness.

The world will remember what we did here. The twin bombings. The declaration of war.

But more than that, they'll remember that we did it together.

And that makes all the difference.

# INTERLUDE
# THE ARCHITECT

## VIKTOR KUZNETSOV

I sit in my office, a glass of vodka untouched on the desk before me, studying the reports with the cold focus that has kept me alive for forty years in this business.

Police station bombing. Volkov mansion destroyed. Coordinated strikes. Professional execution.

Nadia's work. I recognize her signature anywhere. The precision, the timing, the calculated chaos. But this isn't the Nadia I created. The Nadia I molded from a broken sixteen-year-old girl into the perfect weapon wouldn't go rogue. Wouldn't burn evidence that implicates my organization. Wouldn't declare war on everyone.

The Sokolov girl broke her.

I saw it coming, if I'm honest with myself. The moment I gave Nadia that assignment, I knew it was a risk. Kira Sokolov is chaos incarnate, and chaos has a way of spreading. But I underestimated how completely she would infect my best asset.

My phone rings. I answer without looking at the screen. "Report."

"We've tracked them to the industrial district," my lieutenant says. "Three possible locations. Do you want us to move in?"

"No." I lean back in my chair. "Pull back. Let them think they're safe."

"Sir?"

"Nadia knows how we operate. If we push too hard, she'll disappear completely. We need to make her come to us." I take a sip of vodka, finally. "Leak information that we've found the Sokolov family's offshore accounts. Make it look like we're going after Kira's inheritance. She won't be able to resist."

"And if that doesn't work?"

I look at the photograph on my desk. Nadia at seventeen, fresh from her first kill, eyes already dead. I was proud of her then. Proud of what I'd made her.

Now she is my greatest failure.

"Then we burn down every place she's ever felt safe until she has nowhere left to run but to me." I set down the glass. "She was mine for fifteen years. I'm not letting some broken heiress take that away."

I end the call and return to the reports. Somewhere in this city, Nadia and Kira are planning their next move. And I will be ready.

I created the Black Dahlia. I can destroy her too.

# CHAPTER NINE
## KIRA

## SOKOLOV MANSION AMBUSH

The invitation is on black card stock, embossed with gold lettering. The Sokolov family requests the honor of your presence for a reconciliation dinner.

I hold it up to the light in the abandoned apartment where Nadia and I have been hiding for three days. Outside, the city is still reeling from the bombings. Inside, we've been living on stolen food and adrenaline.

And sex. Lots of sex.

"It's a trap," Nadia says without looking up, methodically disassembling her gun at the kitchen table.

"Obviously." I set the invitation down, trace the lettering with one finger. "My grandmother's handwriting. She always did have beautiful penmanship."

Nadia slots the barrel back into place with a click. "You're not going."

I look at her…my Angel, my killer, my salvation. She's wearing just a tank top and tactical pants, her hair pulled back, a bruise on her collarbone from where I bit her last night. She looks dangerous and beautiful and utterly focused.

God, I'm so gone for her.

"I have to go," I say.

"The hell you do."

"The hell I don't." I cross to the table, kneel beside her chair. "This is my family. My blood. I need to face them one last time."

"They'll put a bullet between your eyes before you finish your soup."

"Probably." I smile, but it doesn't reach my eyes. "But I need to look them in the face and tell them I'm not afraid anymore. I need them to know I chose this. I chose you."

Her jaw tightens. She sets down the gun, cups my face in both hands. "Then I'm coming with you."

"They'll kill you too."

"They can stand in line."

This is why I love her. This fierce, protective, utterly insane devotion.

"Okay," I say. "But we do it my way. I go in first, alone. You come in when things go to shit."

"When. Not if."

"Exactly." I grin. "You know me so well."

THE SOKOLOV MANSION LOOKS EXACTLY AS I REMEMBER, all old-world opulence and barely concealed violence. Crystal chandeliers, marble floors, ancestral portraits staring down with dead eyes. The dining room has been set for four: me, my grandmother Zoya, my brother Mikhail, and one empty chair.

The empty chair is for my corpse, probably.

I arrive in a black velvet dress, my hair wild, makeup dark. I look like I'm attending a funeral. In a way, I am.

Mikhail greets me at the door, his smile sharp as broken glass. "Kirasha. You look well."

"Liar." I take his offered arm, feel his grip tighten possessively. "You look like shit, brother."

His smile widens. "I've missed your charm."

I've missed nothing about you.

We walk into the dining room together. Zoya sits at the head of the table, silver-haired and regal, a queen in pearls and poison. She raises her glass as I enter.

"To family," Zoya says. "May we never be divided."

"By what?" I ask, taking my seat. "Greed? Bullets? Love?"

"By ghosts," Zoya replies, her eyes cold. "You've been haunting us long enough, child."

The dinner is excruciating. They make small talk in Russian, old family gossip, veiled threats disguised as concern. I barely touch my food, hyperaware of every sound, every movement.

Mikhail pours wine with one hand, the other resting casually on his hip where I know he keeps a gun.

Zoya smiles, her eyes never leaving my face.

They're waiting. Drawing it out. Making me suffer before they kill me.

"Tell me," Zoya says finally, setting down her fork with deliberate precision. "This woman you've been running with. The Black Dahlia. Is she worth dying for?"

I meet her gaze without flinching. "She's worth living for. That's more than I can say for anyone in this room."

The temperature drops ten degrees.

Mikhail's smile vanishes. "You ungrateful…"

"Psychopath?" I finish. "Disappointment? Waste of perfectly good breeding stock? Come on, **Misha**. You can do better than that."

He stands abruptly, chair scraping across marble. "You should have stayed gone."

"And miss this lovely reunion?" I laugh, the sound bright and brittle. "I wouldn't dream of it."

That's when the men emerge from the shadows.

Six of them, armed, faces hidden behind masks. They've

been waiting in the corners of the room, behind the curtains, in the doorways. Professional. Silent. Deadly.

Right on schedule.

My heart hammers but I don't move, don't flinch. I knew this was coming.

Mikhail pulls his gun, presses it to my temple. "You should have stayed a ghost."

"Funny," I say. "I could have said the same thing about you."

# NADIA

The explosion comes from the kitchen.

Not a bomb…a flashbang, designed to disorient, not kill. I designed it that way. The dining room fills with smoke and noise and chaos. The guards stumble, temporarily blinded.

I come through the smoke like an avenging angel, gun raised, mask covering the lower half of my face. I shoot the first two guards before they can react, and drop a third with a knife to the throat.

This is what I am. What I've always been.

Mikhail spins toward me, gun swinging away from Kira's head. It's the opening she needs.

She grabs a steak knife from the table and drives it into his thigh. He screams and staggers back. Kira lunges for his gun, but another guard grabs her and drags her backward.

I'm already moving. I shoot the guard holding Kira, catch her as she falls, and pull her behind an overturned table.

"Are you hurt?" I demand, my hands running over her body, checking for wounds.

"I'm fine." She's laughing, breathless and manic. "You came."

"Of course I came, you idiot."

More gunfire. The remaining guards are regrouping or taking cover. Mikhail is bleeding and furious, screaming orders. Zoya has disappeared, probably to call rein-forcements.

"We need to move," I say. "Now."

We run, keeping low, using the smoke as cover. I lead us through the service corridors I memorized from the blueprints, shooting anyone who gets in our way. Kira follows, her stolen gun hot in her hands, blood on her dress.

Behind us, Mikhail is still screaming. "Find them! I want them alive!"

Not going to happen.

We burst through a door into the mansion's back gardens. Rain is falling, cold and hard, turning the manicured lawns into mud. We can hear footsteps behind us, shouts, the sound of dogs barking.

"The garage," Kira gasps, pointing.

"No time." I grab her hand, pull her toward the perimeter wall. "We climb."

We scale the wall together, hands slipping on wet stone, bullets whizzing past our heads. I go over first, drop into the alley beyond, then catch Kira as she falls.

We run.

My lungs are burning, my shoulder wound from earlier reopening, and blood is soaking through my shirt. But I don't stop. Can't stop. Not until Kira is safe.

Safe. As if anywhere will be safe for us now.

I APPROACH THE ABANDONED ESTATE DEEP IN THE Serebryany Bor forest, built in 1910 by a merchant family that made their fortune in tea. After the Revolution it was seized, turned into a Communist Party retreat, then abandoned in the '80s when the roof began to collapse. Now it sits among the pines, slowly being reclaimed by nature. The locals call it the

"Ghost Palace." Teenagers dare each other to spend the night. No one ever does.

Nadia told me that three years ago, she found it while running from a job gone wrong. She hid in the ballroom until dawn, surrounded by peeling wallpaper and the ghosts of parties long dead. It felt fitting a palace for ghosts, and she was the biggest ghost of all.

Now she's brought us here, to the place where the old world died, and the new one hasn't quite taken hold. We stumble inside, soaked and shaking. Blood seeps from a graze on my ribs, the bullet having torn through my dress and left a shallow furrow in my skin.

"Sit," Nadia commands, her voice rough.

I collapse onto an old chaise lounge, its velvet rotted and torn. Through half-closed eyes I watch her gather supplies: a first-aid kit she stashed here, bottled water, bandages.

"This is going to hurt," she warns.

"Everything hurts." My laugh is weak. "What's a little more pain?"

She cleans the wound with careful, efficient movements, but her hands are trembling. When she presses the antiseptic-soaked cloth to my skin, I hiss and grab her wrist.

"I'm sorry," she whispers. "I'm so sorry."

"Don't..." I pull her closer, press our foreheads together. "Don't apologize. You saved my life."

"I almost lost you."

"But you didn't." My fingers tangle in her hair. "I'm here. We're here. Together."

Her control finally cracks. She buries her face in my shoulder and shakes, not quite crying but close. All the fear she's been holding back the terror of imagining a world without me pours out in silent tremors.

I hold her, stroke her hair, and murmur in Russian: "Ya tebya lyublyu. Ya tebya lyublyu." I love you. I love you.

When she finally pulls back, her eyes are red but dry. She

finishes bandaging me in silence, then sits beside me on the chaise, our bodies pressed together for warmth.

"Nadia?" I say after a long silence.

"Yeah?"

"Do you think about her? The woman from the club. Svetlana."

Her name lands like a punch to the chest. I've tried not to think about her, but she haunts me differently than the others. The syndicate men, the corrupt officials, they knew the life they'd chosen, they understood the risks. But Svetlana was just a woman at a nightclub, flirting, living her life. Until we decided she shouldn't be.

"Every night," I admit quietly. "I see her eyes. The confusion. She didn't understand why it was happening."

My voice is barely a whisper. "I killed her for you, to prove we were the same. And now I can't stop seeing her face either."

"Do you regret it?"

I'm silent a long moment. When I speak, her voice is raw. "I regret that she had to die. I regret that she was innocent." She looks at me, fierce and haunted. "And that's what makes us monsters, isn't it? Not that we killed her, but that we'd do it again. For each other, we'd burn the whole world without a second thought."

I pull her closer, and we sit in the weight of that truth. We've crossed a line that can never be uncrossed. We're not antiheroes fighting a corrupt system. We're not vigilantes taking down criminals. We're just two broken people whose love has become its own kind of violence.

"I used to tell myself I was different from the men I killed," she says. "That I had rules. That I only killed people who deserved it. But that was a lie I told myself to sleep at night."

"And now?"

"Now I know what I am. What we are." I turn to face her. "We're not the heroes of this story, Kira. We're the cautionary tale, the warning of what happens when love becomes obsession, when devotion becomes destruction."

"I know." I rest my head on her shoulder. "But I still choose you, even knowing what we are. Even knowing how this ends."

"Me too," she whispers. "God help me, me too."

We sit in silence, two monsters holding each other in the ruins of a dead family's mansion, haunted by the ghost of an innocent woman we murdered for nothing more than jealousy and possession. Svetlana deserved better than us. But we're all she had.

"They'll come for us," I say quietly. "My family won't stop until we're dead."

"I know."

"We can't run forever."

"I know."

I turn to look at her, my green eyes serious in the dim light. "Then what do we do?"

NADIA

I'm quiet for a long moment, thinking. My fingers trace the scar on my wrist, a habit from childhood when decisions felt impossible. Then I reach into my jacket and pull out the dossier I've been carrying, the one with all the information we've gathered on both syndicates. The pages are dog-eared, stained with coffee and something darker. Blood, probably mine.

"We don't run," I say, voice steadier than I feel. "We end it. All of it. We burn down both families, leave nothing but ashes."

"That's suicide," Kira says, but her eyes light up the way they did when we first kissed hungry, reckless.

"Maybe." I look at her, memorizing the curve of her jaw, the small scar above her eyebrow. "But at least it's our choice. At least we go out on our terms."

She smiles, wild and beautiful and utterly unafraid. "When do we start?"

"Tomorrow. Tonight, we rest." I pull her closer, wrap us both in an old blanket I found in what was once a servant's quarters. It smells of dust and forgotten lives. "Tonight, we just exist."

We lie together on the ruined chaise as rain drums against broken windows and thunder rolls across the sky. Her head on my chest, my arms around her body, both of us battered and bleeding and impossibly alive. I feel her heartbeat against mine, the rhythm I'd recognize anywhere now.

"Nadia?" she whispers.

"Yeah?"

"If you go, I follow. If you fall, I fall."

I kiss the top of her head, breathe in the scent of her, gunpowder, expensive perfume, and something uniquely Kira. "I know, solnyshko. I know."

We fall asleep like that, two killers finding peace in each other's arms, while outside the city hunts us and our enemies plot our deaths. I dream of her hands, her smile, the way she looked at me across that gallery the first time.

But for now, in this moment, we're safe. We're entwined in each other's warmth, a sanctuary amid the chaos. And that is all we need.

# KIRA

I dream of fire and flowers. Of Nadia's hands on my skin, her lips on my throat. Of a world where we could just be: no families, no violence, no death waiting around every corner.

When I wake, she's already awake, watching me with those gray eyes.

"What are you thinking?" I ask.

"That I've never wanted anything the way I want you," she says quietly. "That I'd burn the whole world down to keep you."

"You already are," I point out.

"I know." She traces my face with her fingers.

I pull her into a kiss. "But we're just getting started."

Tomorrow, we'll plan the final assault. Tomorrow, we'll prepare to die.

But tonight, we're just two women who found each other in the darkness and refused to let go.

And that's the most dangerous thing of all.

# CHAPTER TEN

# NADIA

## RECOVERY AND CONFESSIONS

The derelict mansion smells of rot and rain. Water drips through holes in the ceiling, pooling on warped floorboards that groan with every step. The walls are streaked with mold, the windows shattered, letting in the cold wind that howls through empty rooms like the ghosts of the wealthy family who once lived here.

Now it's just us, hiding from a city that wants us dead.

Kira lies on the chaise lounge, a once-grand piece of furniture now reduced to torn velvet and exposed springs. Her skin is pale as moonlight, fever-flushed, sweat beading on her forehead. The wound in her side has been cleaned and stitched, but infection is setting in despite my best efforts.

I sit beside her, gun in my lap, eyes hollow with exhaustion. I have barely slept in two days, terrified that if I close my eyes, she'll slip away.

"You should rest," she whispers, her voice rough.

"I'm fine."

"Liar." Her hand finds mine, squeezes weakly. "I can feel you shaking."

She's right. I am shaking. Not on the outside where anyone can see, but inside where it matters. The fear of losing her, the weight of what we've done, the certainty that this can't end well, it's all catching up to me.

"I almost lost you," I say quietly. "At the mansion. When Mikhail had that gun to your head, I…" My voice catches. "I saw the world without you in it. And it was empty."

Her eyes fill with tears. "Angel…"

"Don't." I press my fingers to her lips. "Let me finish. I've spent my whole life being empty. Viktor trained me to be a ghost, to move through the world without leaving a mark, without feeling anything. And I was good at it. I was perfect at it."

I pause, brushing a strand of damp hair from her forehead.

"Then you came along and tore through all of that. You made me feel things I didn't know I could feel. You made me want things I'd convinced myself I didn't deserve. You made me alive."

"And you hate me for it," she says, but there's no accusation in her voice. Just understanding.

"No." I lean down, press my forehead to hers. "I love you for it. I love you so much it terrifies me. Because loving you means I have something to lose. And I've never been afraid of dying until now."

Her tears spill over, running down her temples into her hair. "I'm not going to die. Not yet. We have too much left to burn."

I laugh, the sound broken and beautiful. "You're insane."

"I'm learning from the best."

We stay like that for a long moment, breathing the same air, two broken people finding wholeness in each other's damage.

Kira is stronger. Not healthy, she'll probably never be healthy again, not after everything. But strong enough to sit up, to walk around the mansion's dusty rooms, to plan.

But the next morning, reality crashes back in.

We spread the blueprints across the ballroom floor, using candles for light since the electricity was cut decades ago. The

Sokolov headquarters. The Volkov stronghold. Police stations. Safe houses. Every location marked, every weakness identified.

"We hit them all," Kira says, tracing routes with her finger. "One night. Coordinated strikes. We don't give them time to regroup."

I study the maps, my mind already calculating. "It's impossible. We can't be in multiple locations simultaneously."

"So we prioritize." She taps the Sokolov headquarters. "My family first. They're the biggest threat."

"No." I shake my head. "Viktor is the biggest threat. He knows how I think, how I operate. We take him out first, or he'll anticipate every move we make."

Kira's jaw tightens. "My family has more resources. More men. If we don't cripple them immediately…"

"They're already crippled. Your grandmother is possibly injured or dead. Your brother is injured. They're scrambling." I pull out a different map, one showing Viktor's compound. "But Viktor is calm. Collected. He's been planning for this since the moment I went rogue."

"And you think you can outsmart your own mentor?"

"I think I'm the only one who can." I look at her. "He trained me for fifteen years. I know his patterns, his contingencies. But he also knows mine. Which means we need to do something he'd never expect."

"Like what?"

I tap the map. "Viktor always has three escape routes. Always! Front entrance, service exit, underground tunnel to the parking garage. He'll have men at each one, waiting for us to make a move."

"So we don't use the entrances."

"Exactly." I pull out another blueprint, the building's ventilation system. "We go through the roof. Drop down through the air ducts into his office. He won't expect a vertical approach because it's too risky, too exposed."

Kira studies the plans, then looks at me with something like admiration. "That's insane."

"That's why it'll work."

"But the timing…" She traces the route with her finger. "If we hit Viktor first, that gives my family time to fortify their position. By the time we get to them, they'll be ready."

"Not if we make them think we're already there." I pull out my phone, show her a program I've been developing. "We plant devices at the Sokolov headquarters. Timed explosions, motion sensors, automated gunfire. They'll think they're under attack while we're actually hitting Viktor."

Her eyes light up. "A diversion."

"A very loud, very convincing diversion." I zoom in on the Sokolov building's layout. "We plant the devices here, here, and here. Stagger the detonations over twenty minutes. By the time they realize it's automated, we'll be done with Viktor and on our way to finish them."

"What about the police? After the bombing, they'll have every unit in the city on high alert."

"Let them." I pull up traffic camera locations. "We use that. We leak false information about a planned attack on the mayor's residence. Every cop in Moscow will be there, leaving our actual targets exposed."

Kira is quiet for a moment, studying the plans with a tactical eye I didn't know she had. Then she points to a flaw. "Viktor's office has reinforced glass. Bulletproof. We can't shoot our way in from the roof."

"We don't need to." I pull out a small device from my bag, a cutting torch. "We cut a hole. Drop in. He won't have time to react."

"And if he has men in the office with him?"

"He won't. Viktor always meets alone. It's a power play, showing he doesn't need protection." I look at her. "But that's also his weakness. He's so confident in his own invincibility that he's made himself vulnerable."

Kira grins, wild and fierce. "You really have been planning this."

"Since the moment I chose you over him." I start marking timing sequences on the blueprints. "The Sokolov diversion starts at midnight. We hit Viktor at 12:15 while they're distracted. We're in and out in five minutes. Then we move to the Sokolov headquarters at 12:30, while they're still reeling."

"What about extraction? Once we hit the Sokolovs, there's no way out. They'll lock down the whole building."

I meet her eyes. "I know."

Understanding dawns on her face. "This is a one-way mission."

"It always was." I touch her cheek. "But at least we go out on our terms. Together."

She leans into my hand. "I can think of worse ways to die."

"Me too."

We spend the next hour refining the plan, arguing over details, and testing each other's logic. Kira suggests using the service tunnels under the Sokolov building. I point out the security checkpoints. She counters with a plan to disable them remotely. I add a failsafe in case the remote access fails.

It's like a dance, her chaos meeting my precision, her intuition balancing my logic. We're different, but we complement each other perfectly. Two halves of a whole, working in sync.

"You know," Kira says as we finalize the timing sequences, "in another life, we would have made a hell of a team."

"We are a hell of a team."

"I mean legitimately. Like, actual partners. Not..."

I understand what she means. "Maybe. But I think we were always going to end up here. We're too broken for anything else."

"Probably." She looks at the blueprints one more time, then starts rolling them up. "So. Tomorrow night, we die."

"Tomorrow night, we take them all with us."

She grins, and it's the most beautiful, terrible thing I've ever seen. "I wouldn't have it any other way."

Her smile is fierce, devastating. She crawls across the blueprints to kiss me, hard and desperate, tasting like blood and fever and promise.

When we break apart, both breathing hard, she rests her forehead against mine.

# KIRA

We lie tangled together, the room quiet except for our breathing and the distant wail of sirens. Dawn is coming. Our last dawn.

"Nadia?" I whisper.

"Yeah?"

"Do you believe in anything? After, I mean."

She's quiet for so long I think she won't answer. Then: "I used to believe in nothing. That death was just... the end. Darkness. Silence."

"And now?"

Her fingers trace patterns on my skin. "Now I don't know. I want to believe there's something. That this isn't all we get."

I prop myself up on one elbow to look at her. "What would you want it to be? If you could choose."

She considers this, her gray eyes distant. "A garden. With black dahlias. And no violence. No blood. Just... peace. Quiet." She looks at me. "You'd be there. We'd have all the time we never got here."

My throat tightens. "That sounds perfect."

"What about you? What do you think comes after?"

I've thought about death my whole life: courted it, danced with it, dared it to take me. But I've never really thought about what might come after.

"I used to think it was nothing," I admit. "That death was

just the final escape from all of this." I gesture vaguely at the world outside. "But now… I hope it's something. Somewhere we can be together without all the weight. Without the monsters we've become."

"You think we get forgiven? For what we've done?"

"No." I'm honest about that. "I think we pay for it. For all the innocent people caught in our wake. But maybe after we've paid… maybe then we get something else. Something clean."

Nadia pulls me closer. "I like that. The idea that this isn't the end. That we get more than just today."

"Even if it's a fantasy?"

"Especially if it's a fantasy." She kisses my forehead. "I've spent fifteen years believing I was already dead. That I was just a ghost going through the motions. But you made me feel alive again. If there's any justice in the universe, that has to count for something."

I rest my head on her chest, listening to her heartbeat. "Promise me something."

"Anything."

"If there is something after… if we do get that garden with the dahlias… promise you'll find me. That we won't be separated."

Her arms tighten around me. "I promise. I'll find you in whatever comes next. Even if I have to burn through heaven and hell to do it."

I laugh despite the tears streaming down my face. "That's very you."

"I learned from the best."

We hold each other as the sky begins to lighten outside, two damned souls hoping against hope that damnation isn't the end. That somewhere beyond the violence and the blood and the choices we've made, there's a place where we can just be.

Two women who loved each other.

Nothing more, nothing less.

"Nadia?"

"Yeah?"

"I'm not afraid anymore. Of dying, I mean."

"Me neither." She kisses the top of my head. "As long as we go together."

"Always together," I whisper.

THE SUN RISES, PAINTING THE SKY IN SHADES OF PINK AND gold. Our last sunrise. And somehow, knowing we might have another one somewhere else makes it bearable.

"Tell me something true," she whispers. "Something you've never told anyone."

I'm quiet for a long moment, thinking. Then: "My first kill. I was twelve. A foster father who beat us. I killed him to protect my little brother, Alexei."

Her eyes widen. "You never mentioned a brother."

"He died anyway. Two years later, in a fire. I wasn't there to save him." My voice is flat, emotionless, but my hands are shaking. "I've spent my whole life trying to make that death mean something. Trying to convince myself that if I killed enough bad people, it would balance out. That I could earn redemption."

"And now?" she asks softly.

"Now I know there's no redemption. There's just this. Us. And I'd rather have one real thing than a lifetime of lies."

She kisses me again, softer this time. "Your turn. Ask me something."

"Why flowers?" I ask. "You had them in your safe houses even in your bedroom. Drawings, paintings. Sitting in a glass of water on your windowsill."

She smiles, but it's sad. "My mother. She loved them. Had a whole garden of them at our old house, before my father had it torn down. She used to say they were beautiful because they were dark. That there was honesty in darkness."

"What happened to her?"

"He killed her." Her voice is matter-of-fact, but her eyes are haunted. "Not with his hands. With his words, his cruelty, his indifference. She took pills when I was thirteen. I found her in the bathtub, surrounded by petals."

I pull her close, hold her as she shakes with silent sobs.

"I'm sorry," I whisper.

"Don't be. She's why I'm like this. Why I can't be caged, why I burn everything I touch. She taught me that some people are too beautiful for this ugly world. And when I saw your work, the dahlias you left on bodies. I thought maybe you understood that too."

"I do," I say. "I do now."

We hold each other as the candles burn down, as rain drums against the broken windows, as the city hunts us

THAT NIGHT, WE MOVE THROUGH THE MANSION'S EMPTY rooms, gathering what we need. Guns. Ammunition. Knives. The last of the black dahlias, carefully preserved in a stolen vase.

In what was once a bedroom, we find an old mirror, cracked but still reflecting. I stand in front of it, studying my reflection.

"I look like a ghost," I say.

Nadia comes up behind me, wraps her arms around my waist. In the mirror, we look like two halves of the same person, her dark and cold, me pale and burning.

"We're both ghosts," she says. "We died a long time ago. We just didn't know it."

"Then what's this?" I ask, turning in her arms. "What are we?"

"A haunting." She smiles. "We're haunting each other. And when we're gone, we'll haunt this whole city."

I laugh, wild and free. "Promise?"

"Promise."

We make love there, in front of the broken mirror, watching our reflections move together.

She lays me down on the dusty floor, the candlelight casting shadows across my pale skin. She kisses her way down my body, throat, breasts, the soft plane of my stomach. Taking her time, worshipping every scar and imperfection.

My hands fist in her hair when her mouth finally reaches its destination. "God, yes," I breathe, hips lifting to meet her tongue.

She works me slowly, thoroughly, alternating between gentle licks and firm pressure, reading every gasp and moan like a language only we speak. When she adds her fingers, curling them just right, I cry out, my reflection in the broken mirror showing ecstasy fractured into a thousand pieces.

"Don't stop," I beg. "Please don't stop."

She doesn't. She brings me to the edge twice, then over, watching as I shatter beautifully.

Then I'm pulling her up, rolling us over, straddling her hips. "Your turn, Angel."

My hands are everywhere. Breasts, thighs, finally sliding between her legs. I enter her with two fingers, my thumb finding her clit, working her with the same fierce intensity I bring to everything.

She watches our reflections in the cracked mirror: two women, two ghosts, two halves of the same dark soul, moving together in the candlelight. The sight of me above her, wild-haired and beautiful, is almost as intense as the pleasure building inside her.

When she comes, it's with my name on her lips and tears in her eyes.

Afterward, wrapped in an old blanket we found, I trace the brand on her thigh.

"We're bound," I whisper. "Blood and flowers. Death and devotion."

# KIRA

While Nadia sleeps, I find a piece of charcoal in the ruins of the mansion, probably from the old fireplace. I start sketching on the wall, unable to help myself.

I draw us. Nadia and me, tangled together, but instead of bodies, we're made of thorns and petals. The Thorn Queen and The Black Dahlia. Her face is serene, eyes closed, while mine is wild, mouth open in a laugh or a scream, I'm not sure which.

Around us, I sketch the city burning. Not in horror, but in celebration. Flames that look like flowers, smoke that forms the shape of wings.

"What are you drawing?" Nadia's voice comes from behind me.

I don't stop. "Our ending. The way I see it."

She comes to stand beside me, studying the charcoal sketch. "We're dying."

"We're transforming," I add more detail to the flames. "Death isn't an ending. It's just... a different kind of becoming."

"That's very poetic for someone who's about to commit suicide by syndicate."

I laugh. "I'm an artist. Everything's poetic if you frame it right." I finish the sketch, step back to look at it. "Do you think anyone will find this? After?"

"Maybe. If the building doesn't collapse first."

"Good." I sign it in the corner, just a K with a small dahlia beside it. "I want them to know. That we chose this. That it wasn't a tragedy, it was art."

Nadia wraps her arms around me from behind, resting her chin on my shoulder. "You're insane."

"I know." I lean back against her. "But you love me, anyway."

"I do." She kisses my neck. "Even though you're drawing our death on a wall like it's a museum piece."

"Especially because of that." I turn in her arms. "Promise me something. When we die, when they find our bodies, make sure there are dahlias. Lots of them. I want it to be beautiful."

"It will be," she promises. "I'll make sure of it."

We stand there, looking at the charcoal sketch of our ending, and somehow it makes everything bearable. Because if we can turn our death into art, then maybe it means something. Maybe we're not just two broken people destroying everything we touch.

Maybe we're creating something that will outlast us.

# NADIA

We fall asleep, tangled together, listening to the rain and the distant sirens and the sound of each other's breathing.

For now, in this moment, we're safe.

For now, we have each other.

And that's enough.

When I wake, Kira is already up, dressed in black, checking her weapons with practiced efficiency. The fever is gone, replaced by a manic energy that makes her eyes shine.

"Ready?" she asks, turning to look at me.

I sit up, study the woman I've chosen over everything…my salvation and my damnation, my mirror and my opposite.

"Yes," I say. "Let's finish this."

We load our weapons, tuck black dahlias into our jackets, and walk out of the derelict mansion into the gray morning.

Behind us, the building stands like a monument to our love…broken, beautiful, haunted.

Ahead of us, the city waits, unaware that two of its most dangerous daughters are about to declare war on everything.

I take Kira's hand as we walk toward the car we stole.

"If you go, I follow," she says quietly.

"If you fall, I fall," I reply.

We drive into the city, into the chaos, into the end.

Together.

Always together.

# KIRA

As we drive through the early morning streets, I watch Nadia's profile. The set of her jaw, the way her hands grip the steering wheel, the determination in her eyes.

This is it. The beginning of the end.

I'm not afraid. I should be, we're driving toward certain death, toward a battle we can't win, toward an ending that will be written in blood and fire.

But with her beside me, I feel invincible.

"What are you thinking?" she asks, glancing at me.

"That I'm glad it's you," I say. "That if I have to die, I'm glad I get to do it with you."

Her hand finds mine, squeezes. "We're not dead yet."

"No," I agree. "Not yet."

We drive on, the city waking around us, unaware of the storm coming.

And I smile, wild and free, because for the first time in my life, I'm exactly where I'm supposed to be.

With her.

Always with her.

Until the last breath.

THREE DAYS PASSED IN THE DERELICT MANSION. THREE DAYS of planning, healing, and preparing for what comes next. We know we can't hide forever. The city is hunting us, and eventually, they'll find us.

So we decide to make the first move.

# INTERLUDE
## The Investigator

DETECTIVE IRINA MARKOVIC

I stood in the ruins of the police evidence room, ash and debris crunching under my boots. The explosion had ripped out two floors and killed four officers. Good people. People with families. And for what? To destroy evidence? To send a message?

I'd been hunting the Black Dahlia for three years, ever since that first body turned up with the signature flower. At first, I'd thought it was mob cleanup, professional hits, no witnesses, always clean. But the more I dug, the more I saw something else at work: something personal in the way the bodies were arranged, the care taken with each kill.

The Black Dahlia wasn't just a hired gun. She was an artist. And now she had a partner.

I pulled out my phone and scrolled through the crime-scene photos from the past month: the Volkov gala, the twin bombings, the Sokolov mansion ambush. The body count was climbing, but the pattern had shifted. Where the Black Dahlia had once been surgical and precise, now there was rage. Passion. Chaos.

Kira Sokolov The Thorn Queen did this to her.

I'd read Kira's psychiatric files, sealed juvenile records, and hospital reports. The girl was brilliant and broken in equal measure, a genius with no impulse control and a death wish she'd been nursing since childhood. Put her together with a trained assassin, and you got exactly this: a blood-soaked rampage across Moscow with no end in sight.

My phone buzzed. A text from my informant in the Sokolov organization:

> They're planning something big. Final stand.
> Soon.

I typed back:

> Location?

The reply came immediately:

> Don't know. But when it happens, you'll know.
> The whole city will know.

I pocketed my phone and took in the destroyed evidence room one more time. Four officers are dead. Dozens injured. Millions in damage. And for what? Love, I realized with bitter irony. All of this for love.

I'd spent my career hunting killers, but I'd never seen anything like this, two women so consumed by each other they'd burn the world down rather than be separated. It would almost be romantic if it weren't so fucking tragic.

"Detective?" One of my officers approached, holding a tablet. "We've got surveillance footage from the night of the bombing. You need to see this."

I took the tablet and watched the grainy video: a figure in a security uniform planting the device. Her face was partially obscured, but I saw enough.

There you are.

The Black Dahlia. In the flesh. After three years of chasing shadows, I finally had her on camera.

But it didn't matter. Deep in my gut, I knew this wouldn't

end with an arrest. It was going to end with bodies. Lots of them. The only question was whether I'd be one of them.

I handed back the tablet. "Put out an APB. Armed and extremely dangerous. Do not engage without backup."

"Yes, ma'am."

I stepped out of the ruined building into the cold Moscow night. Somewhere out there, two women were planning their final stand. And I would be there to meet them.

One way or another, this ends soon.

# INTERLUDE
## THE MAKING OF THE WEAPON

### NADIA

#### FIFTEEN YEARS AGO

I'm sixteen years old, and I've just killed a man with my bare hands.

Viktor stands over the body, studying it with the clinical detachment of a surgeon examining his work. "Sloppy," he says. "You hesitated. Hesitation gets you killed."

My hands are shaking. There's blood under my fingernails, on my clothes, in my hair. The man, I don't even know his name, stares at nothing with dead eyes.

"I didn't hesitate," I lie.

Viktor looks at me then, really looks at me, and I see something in his eyes that might be disappointment or might be satisfaction. "You did. For three seconds, you considered letting him live. I saw it."

"He was begging…"

"They always beg." Viktor crouches down, picks up the garrote wire I'd dropped. "That's what separates you from them. They beg because they believe their lives matter more than their choices. You don't beg because you understand the truth."

"What truth?"

"That we're all dead already. Some of us just haven't stopped moving yet." He hands me the wire. "Again. And this time, don't think. Just act."

He brings in another man: bound, gagged, terrified. I don't ask where Viktor gets them. I don't ask what they've done. I just do what I'm told.

Because Viktor saved me. Pulled me from the foster system after I killed that man who hurt my brother. Gave me purpose when I had nothing. Made me into something more than a broken girl with blood on her hands.

He made me the Black Dahlia.

# NADIA - PRESENT DAY

The memory surfaces as I stand in the hotel suite, preparing for our final stand. Fifteen years since Viktor found me. Fifteen years of being his perfect weapon.

And now I'm turning that weapon against him.

My phone rings. Unknown number, but I know who it is. I've been expecting this call.

"Nadia." Viktor's voice is calm, controlled. The same voice that's guided me through a hundred kills. "We need to talk."

"There's nothing to talk about."

"I think there is." A pause. "You're making a mistake. This girl…she's broken you. Made you forget what you are."

"No." I look at Kira, sleeping in the bed, her wild hair spread across the pillow. "She made me remember what I am. What I was before you found me."

"A scared child who killed her foster father?" Viktor's voice hardens. "That's what you were. I made you into something more. Something perfect."

"You made me into a ghost."

"I made you into a survivor." He sighs, and for the first

time, I hear something like emotion in his voice. "I pulled you from the darkness, Nadia. Gave you purpose. Direction. And this is how you repay me?"

"You didn't save me, Viktor. You just taught me how to weaponize my trauma." I grip the phone tighter. "I was sixteen. I was broken and alone and you turned me into a killer. You didn't give me a choice."

"I gave you the only choice that mattered: to be the blade or the victim. You chose the blade."

"Because you made me think those were the only options!" My voice cracks. "But Kira showed me there's a third option. To be human. To feel something other than emptiness."

"And look where that's gotten you." Viktor's voice turns cold. "Hunted. Desperate. About to die in a room for a woman who's as broken as you are."

"Maybe." I smile despite myself. "But at least I'll die feeling something real. That's more than I had with you."

Silence stretches across the line. Then: "I trained you better than this."

"I know. That's why you'll lose." I hang up, my thumb pressing the red button harder than necessary.

The mattress shifts behind me. Kira's voice, still thick with sleep: "Viktor?"

I nod without turning around, my back still to her. "He wanted to remind me what I am."

The sheets rustle as she sits up. Her chin rests on my shoulder, her wild hair tickling my neck. "And what did you tell him?"

"That I'm not his weapon anymore." My voice catches. I feel her arms slide around my waist, her chest warm against my back.

"Good," she whispers against my skin. "Because that's the only version of you I want."

I lean into her embrace, eyes closed, the phone still

clutched in my hand. Viktor's voice echoes: I made you into something perfect.

But he was wrong. He made me into something empty. Kira made me whole.

And if that means dying today, so be it.

# CHAPTER ELEVEN

# NADIA

## THE FINAL ASSAULT

The Sokolov headquarters stands like a glass monument to greed at midnight, reflecting Moscow's skyline in its mirrored facade. The building is a fortress of steel and glass, twenty stories of syndicate power condensed into architecture. Security cameras track every angle. Motion sensors guard every entrance. Armed patrols circle the perimeter on fifteen-minute intervals.

But I've memorized every weakness.

I move through empty corridors with C-4 in my hands, my footsteps silent on marble floors that cost more than most people earn in a lifetime. Behind me, Kira follows, her breathing controlled, her movements precise. We've rehearsed this a dozen times in the abandoned mansion, walking through imaginary hallways, timing each placement to the second.

Now it's real.

The building's skeleton is laid bare in my mind: load-bearing walls on the third, seventh, and fifteenth floors. Structural weaknesses where the architect prioritized aesthetics over integrity. The server room in the basement is where they keep their digital records. The vault on the twelfth floor where they store physical evidence of every crime, every deal, every betrayal.

Viktor taught me this: how to read a building like a body, how to find the places that make it collapse. How to turn architecture into a weapon.

It's fitting that I use his training to destroy what's left of Kira's past.

We reach the ballroom on the third floor. The space is enormous, designed for the parties where the Sokolovs parade their power. Crystal chandeliers hang from the ceiling like frozen tears. The walls are lined with mirrors, making the room seem infinite.

Kira stops in the center, staring up at the chandeliers. Her hand trembles as she pulls out the first charge.

"This one's for the ballroom," she whispers, her voice tight. "Where they paraded me like a prize. Where they introduced me to the men who bid on me like I was livestock."

I move beside her, closing my hands over hers to steady them. Her skin is cold despite the warmth of the building. "Timer's set for 12:15. We'll be with Viktor when it goes off."

"They'll think we're attacking here. By the time they realize…"

"We'll already be gone." My voice sounds flat, matter-of-fact, but my heart is racing. This is the point of no return. Once we set these charges, there's no walking away. "Or dead."

She looks at me then, and I see something fierce burning in her green eyes. Not fear. Not hesitation. Something closer to exhilaration. "Either way, they burn."

Her smile twists something in my chest, pride, maybe, or fear. Or love wearing a mask of violence. I've spent weeks watching her transform from the wild, self-destructive woman I was sent to kill into this: someone with purpose, with direction, with a reason to channel all that beautiful chaos.

Did I make her into this? Or maybe she made herself, and I just gave her permission.

We move through the building like ghosts. At each location, I place the charges with surgical precision while Kira leaves a black dahlia, its petals dark as bruises, dark as the space where innocence used to live. She arranges them carefully, almost reverently, as if she's decorating graves that haven't been dug yet.

"Do you think anyone will understand?" she asks as we move to the fourth floor. "The flowers. What they mean."

"Does it matter?"

"I want them to know it was us. That we chose this."

I pause at the stairwell, checking my watch. We're three minutes ahead of schedule. "They'll know. The whole city will know."

The security guard finds us on the third floor, emerging from the stairwell just as we're finishing the placement near the executive offices.

He's young, maybe twenty-five, with the soft face of someone who hasn't seen real violence yet. Probably working this shift to pay for university, or to support a family, or just because he needed a job, and this one paid well enough not to ask questions.

He opens his mouth to shout, and I'm already moving.

My training takes over. Three steps to close the distance. My hand clamps over his mouth before sound can form. The knife finds the gap between his ribs with practiced precision, angled up toward the heart. He struggles for perhaps five seconds, his eyes wide with shock and terror and the dawning realization that this is how he dies.

I lower him gently to the floor, my hand still over his mouth as the light leaves his eyes. I count his final heartbeats, fourteen of them and then he's gone.

"I'm sorry," I whisper to the corpse.

And I am sorry. Not sorry enough to stop, not sorry enough to turn back, but sorry nonetheless. Viktor would have felt nothing. He would have seen only an obstacle removed, a problem solved. That's how I know she's changed me, I can still feel the weight of taking a life, even when it's necessary. Even when it's survival.

Kira kneels beside me, places a dahlia on his chest with surprising gentleness. "Collateral damage."

"We're all collateral damage," I say, standing. My hands are steady, but something inside me trembles. "Come on. We're out of time."

We finish the remaining placements in silence, each lost in our own thoughts. By the time we reach the service exit, we've planted seven charges throughout the building, each one timed to detonate in sequence, creating a cascade of destruction that will bring the entire structure down.

Seven charges. Seven dahlias. Seven deaths we've chosen.

We slip out through the service exit, disappearing into the Moscow night. Behind us, the building stands pristine and oblivious, lit up against the darkness, waiting for its immolation.

Waiting for us to destroy it from within, just like they tried to destroy Kira.

# KIRA

Viktor's compound looms on the city's fringe like a Stalinist stronghold—harsh concrete, razor wire, and an army of cameras feeding into a hundred watchful eyes. Guards patrol in pairs, routes overlapping so no corner stays dark for more than thirty seconds. It openly declares: I have enemies, and I'm prepared.

Yet three years ago Nadia helped draw these blueprints when she was still his perfect weapon. She mapped the gaps in the lighting, timed the shifting patrols, and planted fail-safes— hidden flaws to exploit if Viktor ever turned on her.

That day is here.

We slip in from the north, where a single floodlight leaves a sliver of shadow between wall and building. Nadia moves first, low and silent. I follow, heart hammering. She freezes, holds up three fingers—three minutes until the next patrol creeps near.

We circle to an east-wing service ladder and climb in silence. At the top, Nadia produces a diamond cutter and etches a perfect circle into the reinforced skylight. Below, gravel crunches, radios chatter. Seconds tick away.

Viktor Kuznetsov sits at his desk, backlit by his computer. He's grayer, more lined than the files showed but those eyes remain: unblinking, cold, hungry for control.

My hatred burns hotter than any pain I've known. This is the man who stole fifteen years of her life, who cut out her humanity and sold her perfection.

Nadia drops the glass panel aside. He doesn't look up. We clip our rope to the anchor, load our weapons her pistol, my knife and exchange a look. In her eyes, a flicker of what comes after. I squeeze her hand. "I'm here."

She steels herself. "On three."

At 12:14 AM, we lower through the skylight. Glass shatters in a soft shower as we land beside his desk, angels of reckoning.

He's waiting.

"Nadia," he says, as if welcoming a guest. "I wondered when you'd return."

She raises her pistol. "I'm here to end this."

His thin smile never reaches his eyes as they drift to me. "And you," he says with contempt, "The Thorn Queen herself. Sokolov princess turned savior." He leans forward slightly. "Do you even know what she truly is?"

"She was human," I say. "Not your property."

He chuckles. "I found her feral, starving. I perfected her."

"She was empty. I taught her to live."

He leans forward, that old pride glinting. "Kill me, and you prove you're still mine. Come back to me."

The first explosion rattles the windows, the Sokolov investments blowing sky-high on cue. Flames paint the sky orange.

"A diversion," Viktor hisses.

"She's not yours," I reply. "She never was."

His old confidence wavers. "You know what this means, suicide."

"We died the moment we chose each other," I say.

He studies Nadia, as if recognizing her for the first time. "You were perfect."

"Perfect weapons are hollow," she breathes. Her finger tightens. "Goodbye, Viktor."

The shot is quiet.

He slumps over the desk, eyes wide in final surprise. Nadia stands frozen, pistol still raised. I step forward and lift a single black dahlia from my coat pocket. We place the flower on his chest. Its petals wilt in the cool air.

Sirens wail outside. The city awakens to our work.

She exhales, hollow and raw. "It's done."

"One more target," I say softly.

She straightens, force returning. "Then the reckoning."

# NADIA

The penthouse is exactly as Kira described, a secret safe house the Sokolov family kept for emergencies, known only to the inner circle. She spent summers here as a child, she told me once, her voice distant with memory. Playing in rooms designed for hiding, for disappearing when the world got too dangerous.

She learned to be invisible here. Learned that survival meant making herself small.

Now it will be their tomb.

We arrive at 1:00 AM, using the service elevator and the security codes Kira stole from her grandmother's safe two years ago. The codes still work; arrogance or oversight, it doesn't matter. We're in.

The lights are on. Two figures wait in the living room, silhouetted against the floor-to-ceiling windows that overlook the city.

Kira's grandmother Zoya and her brother Mikhail, the last survivors of the family that sold her, that watched her suffer and called it business. That treated her like a commodity to be traded for power and influence.

Zoya sits in a high-backed chair like a throne, silver-haired and regal, a queen in pearls and poison. Mikhail stands beside her, his hand resting casually on the back of her chair. They're dressed formally, as if this is a dinner party and not an execution.

"Kirusha," Zoya says, using her childhood name. Her voice is cold, controlled, the same voice that ordered hits and arranged marriages and decided the fates of hundreds. "Come home. We can forget all this."

Kira laughs, high and wild, a sound that raises the hair on my arms. "Forget? You want me to forget?"

"We did what we had to do," Zoya says, her voice cold. Not apologetic. Not regretful. Simply stating fact. "For the family. You understand family, don't you?"

"I understand what you did to me." Kira's gun is already in her hand, rising with terrible purpose. "I understand perfectly."

Mikhail moves then, reaching for his own weapon, but I'm faster. I've been waiting for this, anticipating his response. My knife is already in my hand.

What follows is not a fight. It's a ritual, a dance choreographed in blood and fury.

I move like water, fluid, inevitable. Viktor trained me for this, though he never imagined I'd use it against his allies. Mikhail dies first, my knife finding his throat, but not before his gun clears his holster. His eyes go wide with betrayal, with the shock of being killed by someone he never saw as a threat.

I feel nothing. No satisfaction, no remorse. Just the mechanical efficiency of a weapon doing what it was made to do.

But then I look at Kira, and I feel everything.

She's fire incarnate, wild, consuming, beautiful in her rage. Zoya tries to run, moving with surprising speed for her age, but Kira is faster. The first shot takes her in the back, sending her sprawling. The second is to the head, execution-style, ensuring there's no chance of survival.

The matriarch who orchestrated everything, who sold her granddaughter and called it family duty, begging at the end. And Kira listens to every word before pulling the trigger.

Silence falls like ash.

We stand in the carnage, breathing hard, the reality of what we've done settling over us like a shroud. This is different from the others. These aren't syndicate enemies or corrupt officials. This is Kira's blood, her family, the people who raised her.

And she killed them without hesitation.

We place black dahlias on each body, arranging them like offerings on an altar. The flowers look obscene against the expensive carpet, against the backdrop of wealth and privilege.

"This is for her," I whisper to Mikhail's corpse, though I'm not sure who I mean, Kira, or the girl she used to be, or the woman we've both become in the crucible of revenge.

# KIRA

I stand in the center of the carnage, breathing hard, blood on my face and hands. Mikhail's blood. Zoya's blood. My family's blood.

I should feel horror. Disgust. The weight of what I've done crush down on me.

Instead, I feel transcendent. Terrible. Free.

"Let it all burn," I say, my voice steady despite the trembling in my hands.

I pull out the lighter Nadia gave me, a silver Zippo engraved with a dahlia. I flick it open, hold the flame to the curtains. The fabric catches immediately, spreading with hungry eagerness. I watch it climb the walls, consuming the room where I once played as a child, where I was still innocent enough to believe my family loved me.

Where I learned that love was transactional and I was worth only what I could bring them.

"We need to leave," Nadia says, but I can't move. I'm transfixed, watching the flames devour my past, watching the penthouse that held so many painful memories begin to burn.

"Not yet. Let me watch. Just for a moment."

She waits, one hand on my shoulder, while the fire consumes everything. The heat is intense, the smoke already thick, but I feel peaceful. Almost serene.

This is what closure looks like. Not forgiveness. Not understanding. Just fire and ash and the satisfaction of watching it all burn.

"Okay," I say finally, tearing my eyes away from the flames. "I'm ready."

We run.

# NADIA

The service tunnels beneath Moscow are a maze of Soviet-era infrastructure, steam pipes and electrical conduits, forgotten passages that connect the city's underbelly. I've mapped them over years of operations, memorizing every turn, every exit, every place where the old city meets the new.

I navigate by memory and instinct, pulling Kira through the darkness while sirens wail overhead. Our footsteps echo on concrete, our breathing harsh in the enclosed space. Behind us, I can hear the distant sound of the penthouse burning, of emergency services mobilizing.

We're both wounded. Kira took a bullet in the shoulder during the penthouse fight, Mikhail got a shot off before I killed him. Blood leaves a trail behind us, but we don't stop, can't stop, not until we reach the hotel.

The luxury suite is exactly as we left it, champagne on ice, silk sheets turned down, a sanctuary purchased with the last of Kira's offshore accounts. We stumble inside and barricade the door with furniture, then collapse against each other.

We're laughing and weeping, high on adrenaline and the certainty of death.

I press a towel to her shoulder, trying to stop the bleeding. My hands are shaking now, the adrenaline wearing off, leaving behind exhaustion and pain. "They'll find us. They're probably already on their way."

"I know." Her smile is radiant despite the pain, despite the blood soaking through her dress. "But we have tonight."

"Tonight, and then…"

"And then we go together. Like we promised."

I pull her close, careful of her wounds, and press our foreheads together. Outside, the city is mobilizing police, surviving gangsters, and everyone who wants us dead. But in this room, in this moment, we're untouchable.

"Together," I whisper. "Always together."

# KIRA

She kisses me, and I taste blood and smoke and something sweeter, freedom, maybe, or the peace that comes with accepting the inevitable.

We've burned our world down, and now we'll burn with it.

But first, we have tonight.

First, these hours where our pulses still hammer against each other's skin.

The world will take us tomorrow, but it cannot have this.

First, these hours where our pulses still hammer against each other's skin.

# CHAPTER TWELVE
## NADIA

### THE DEATH PACT

The luxury hotel suite sits like a crown jewel sixty floors above the city, glass walls offering a panoramic view of Moscow's glittering sprawl. But tonight, the opulence is marred by violence, overturned furniture barricades the door, and blood spatters across white marble floors. The air is thick with gun oil, sweat, and the fading sweetness of expensive perfume.

Outside, the city has mobilized its full fury. Police spotlights sweep across the building's facade like searchlights hunting prey. Sirens wail in an endless chorus. SWAT teams assemble in the lobby below, their radios crackling with tactical chatter. What remains of both syndicates, Sokolov loyalists and Volkov survivors, have joined forces for once, united by a single purpose: kill the women who destroyed their world.

Inside the suite, Kira and I prepare for our final stand.

I stand at the window, silhouetted against the city lights, my reflection a ghost in the glass. Blood from a shoulder wound has soaked through my black shirt, but I barely feel it anymore. Pain has become background noise, drowned out by the clarity that comes with accepting the inevitable.

Behind me, I hear Kira moving, the rustle of fabric, the soft clink of ammunition being loaded into magazines. We've been preparing for an hour, working in companionable silence, each lost in our own thoughts.

"How many do you think are down there?" she asks, her voice surprisingly steady.

I don't turn from the window. "Enough."

"Good." Her laugh is soft, almost wistful. "I'd hate for this to be easy."

I finally look back. She sits cross-legged on the bed, surrounded by weapons, two pistols, a knife, extra magazines, the last of our black dahlias arranged in a careful row. She's changed into a simple black dress, her wild auburn hair pulled back from her face. Without makeup, with her features softened by candlelight, she looks younger. Almost innocent.

Almost.

"Come here," she says, patting the bed beside her.

I cross the room, my boots crunching on broken glass. I sit, and she immediately begins tending to my shoulder wound, her hands gentle despite the circumstances.

"You should have let me stitch this earlier," she murmurs, cleaning the wound with vodka from the minibar.

"We didn't have time."

"We have time now." Her eyes meet mine, green and fierce. "All the time in the world."

The irony isn't lost on either of us. We have hours at most, maybe less.

I watch her work, memorizing every detail: the way her brow furrows in concentration, the delicate bones of her wrists, the old scars that crisscross her pale skin like a map of survival. I think about the first time I saw her, laughing at that Sokolov party, burning money and breaking things just to watch the world react.

I was sent to kill this woman. Instead, I fell in love with her.

Not love, Viktor's voice whispers in my head. Obsession. Madness. Codependency born of shared trauma and violence.

But as Kira finishes stitching and presses a kiss to the bandaged wound, I know the truth. It is love. Dark, consuming, probably doomed from the start. But real.

"Your turn," I say, reaching for her arm where a bullet grazed her during our escape from the warehouse.

We switch positions, and I clean and bandage with the same careful attention. When I finish, I don't let go. I hold her hand, studying the contrast between my pale fingers and hers. Both stained with blood, both marked by the dahlia brands we gave each other.

"Tell me something true," she whispers, echoing the words she's spoken before. "Something you've never told anyone."

I'm quiet for a long moment, thinking. Then: "I used to dream about dying. Not suicide, just... disappearing. Becoming nothing. I thought it would be peaceful."

"And now?"

"Now I might be terrified of it." My voice cracks. "Because dying means leaving you. And I've never wanted to stay alive so badly."

Her eyes fill with tears. She pulls me close, pressing our foreheads together. "I was never alive until you saw me. Every breath before you was just... existing. Surviving. But not living."

We stay like that, breathing in sync, two broken people finding wholeness in each other's damage.

"I don't want to die," she admits, her voice small.

"Neither do I."

"But we will."

"Yes."

The truth hangs between us, heavy and undeniable. We've burned too many bridges, killed too many people, and made too many enemies. There's no escape route, no last-minute reprieve. This is the end we chose when we decided to burn the world down together.

"Then let's make it count," she says, pulling back to look at me. Her tears have stopped, replaced by that familiar wild light. "Let's make them remember us."

I smile. A real smile, not the cold mask I wore for so many years. "They'll remember. I promise."

# KIRA

We spend the next hour preparing. Checking weapons. Loading magazines. Discussing tactics with the same clinical precision we brought to every job. But underneath the professionalism is something else. A desperate need to touch, to reassure, to memorize.

Every time we pass each other, our hands brush. Lips meet in brief, fierce kisses. Words are spoken and left unfinished, because what is there left to say?

As midnight approaches, we stand together at the window, watching the police activity below. More vehicles have arrived, armored trucks, tactical units, and a mobile command center. The entire city has come to witness our end.

She kisses me then, deep and desperate, trying to pour everything she can't say into that single gesture. I love you. I'm sorry. Thank you. Forgive me.

When we break apart, we're both crying.

"Make love to me," I whisper. "One last time."

# NADIA

We move to the bed, undressing each other with trembling hands. I unzip her blood-red dress, letting it fall away. She unbuttons my shirt, her fingers lingering on each revealed inch of skin. The city lights paint our naked bodies in shades of gold and shadow.

I lay her back against the pillows, taking my time. I kiss every scar, the one on her shoulder, the brand on her ribs, the old cuts on her wrists. "I love every part of you," I whisper against her skin. "Even the broken parts. Especially those."

Her hands roam my body, memorizing the feel of me. When my fingers slide inside her, she gasps, her back arching off the bed. "Slower," she breathes. "I want this to last."

I move with aching slowness, each stroke deliberate, drawing out her pleasure until she's trembling, begging. Only then do I increase my pace, my thumb circling her clit while my fingers curl inside her.

She comes with my name broken on her lips, her nails raking down my back hard enough to draw blood.

Then she's pushing me onto my back, settling between my thighs. "I want to taste you," she murmurs. "One last time."

Her mouth is exquisite, warm and wet and skilled. My fingers tangle in her auburn hair, guiding her, losing myself in the sensation. When she adds her fingers, filling me completely, I feel tears slip down my temples.

"You're mine," I gasp as the pleasure builds. "God, Kira, you're mine."

She looks up at me, eyes bright with tears and devotion. "I know, solnyshko. I know."

When I come, it's with a broken cry, my body convulsing, pleasure and grief indistinguishable.

We lie tangled together afterward, hearts racing, skin slick with sweat and tears. Her head rests on my chest, listening to my heartbeat slow. Neither of us speaks, there are no words left that matter.

"I love you," she says. The first time she's said it without laughter or irony.

"I love you," I reply. The first time I've said it at all.

We hold each other as the night deepens, listening to the sounds of preparation outside. The calm before the storm. The last peace we'll ever know.

# KIRA

The first light of dawn paints the sky in shades of pink and gold. It would be beautiful if it wasn't also our death sentence.

Nadia wakes first, though I don't think she really slept. I can feel her watching me in the darkness, memorizing my face.

I open my eyes and meet her gaze. "It's time?"

"Soon."

I rise, moving to stand beside her. Together, we look out at the city...this place that made us, broke us, and now will bury us.

"Was it worth it?" she asks, her voice barely audible. "Everything we burned?"

I trace the outline of her jaw with my fingertip. "I'd burn it all again."

We dress together, a ritual of preparation. I choose a blood-red dress, "If I'm going to die, I'm going to look fucking magnificent doing it", and she helps me zip it up. We braid each other's hair, her fingers gentle on my scalp, my hands steady as I weave her dark locks into something manageable.

Finally, we each tuck a black dahlia into our clothes, mine in my hair, hers in her jacket pocket, right over her heart.

"Together?" I ask, holding out my hand.

"Always," she replies, taking it.

# CHAPTER THIRTEEN

# Nadia

## THE FINAL STAND

We move to the center of the room, positioning ourselves back-to-back, guns loaded and ready. The barricade at the door is already shaking. I can hear the battering ram, the shouted orders, the countdown to breach.

"I'm not afraid," Kira whispers.

"Neither am I," I lie. I'm terrified. Not of dying, but of failing her in these final moments. Of not being enough.

"Liar," she says, but there's affection in her voice. "But I love you, anyway."

The door explodes inward.

Time seems to slow as the first wave of tactical officers pours through the doorway. My training takes over: target acquisition, breath control, and squeeze the trigger. One down. Two. Three.

Beside me, Kira is laughing, that wild, manic sound that first drew me to her. She fires with less precision but equal ferocity, her movements almost dance-like as she dodges and weaves.

The room fills with smoke and noise and chaos. Bullets tear through the air, shattering what remains of the windows. Glass rains down like deadly snow. Blood pools on the marble floors, some ours, most not.

We fight as we've lived these past weeks…in perfect, terrible synchrony. When I need to reload, she covers me. When she stumbles, I catch her. We move as one organism, two halves of a whole, dancing our final dance.

But we're only human. And humans, no matter how skilled or determined, can't fight forever.

I feel the first bullet hit my side: a burning impact that steals my breath. I stumble, and Kira is there immediately, pulling me behind an overturned couch.

"How bad?" she demands, her hands already assessing the wound.

"Bad enough." I cough, tasting copper. "But not yet. Not yet."

We return fire, but more officers are pouring in now. The room is becoming a killbox, and we're the targets.

Kira takes a bullet to the thigh, crying out. I drag her further back, toward the bedroom, buying us precious seconds. But we both know…this is it. The end we've been racing toward since that first moment our eyes met across a crowded party.

# KIRA

We collapse together behind the bed, backs against the wall, guns running low on ammunition. Blood soaks our clothes, our hands, the floor beneath us. The sounds of the assault are deafening: shouting, gunfire, the crunch of boots on broken glass.

I turn to look at Nadia, and despite everything: the pain, the fear, the certainty of death. I'm smiling.

"I meant what I said," I gasp. "About you being worth it."

"I know." She reaches for me, our fingers intertwining.

"Promise me something?"

"Anything."

"Promise me they'll remember us. Not as victims or monsters, but as… us. Together."

She looks at the black dahlias we scattered across the room, at the blood and the broken glass and me, the woman she loves more than life itself.

"They'll remember," she says. "I promise."

More footsteps. More shouting. We're out of time.

I pull out my last weapon: the mother-of-pearl handled knife I've carried since the beginning. She still has one bullet left in her pistol.

We look at each other, a thousand words passing between us in silence. I think of Svetlana, of the innocent life we took. That's the weight we carry into whatever comes next. The price we'll pay.

Then I lean in, pressing my lips to hers in one final, perfect kiss.

"Together?" I whisper against her mouth.

"Always."

# NADIA

In the end, we choose our own ending. Not captured, not executed, not torn apart. Together, as we promised.

She presses the blade to my heart. I press the gun to her temple.

"Together," we say in unison. "Always together."

And then…

The world explodes in light and sound and pain, but it doesn't matter because I'm holding her hand and she's holding mine and we're together, we're together, we're…

# EPILOGUE

# Legends Never Die

The bodies were found entwined, hands still clasped, black dahlias scattered around them like an offering. The city would spend weeks cleaning up the carnage, months investigating, years trying to understand.

But some things can't be understood. Some loves are too dark, too consuming, too fierce to be contained by logic or law.

Detective Markovic stood over the bodies, her face grim. She'd chased these women for weeks, studied their patterns, tried to predict their moves. And in the end, they'd won, not by escaping, but by refusing to be anything other than what they were.

"Close their eyes," she said quietly to the medical examiner. "They've earned that much."

Years later, in dive bars and underground clubs, people still told the story. The Black Dahlia and the Thorn Queen. The assassin and the heiress. The two women who loved each other so fiercely that they burned the world down rather than live in it separately.

A mural appeared on a wall in the old industrial district: two women embracing, surrounded by black dahlias, their faces serene. Beneath it, someone had spray-painted: Some loves are written in blood.

The city tried to forget, but the city never forgets.

On certain nights, when the rain falls and the streets are empty, people swear they can hear laughter echoing through the alleys. Wild, manic, free. And sometimes, in the morning, they find black dahlias scattered where no flowers should grow.

Legends never die. They just wait in the shadows, reminding us that love: real, true, consuming love, is the most dangerous force in the world.

And somewhere, in whatever comes after, Nadia and Kira dance on, bound by blood and flowers, death and devotion.

Together.

Always together.

## *Final Thoughts - The Moment Before*

# KIRA

*This is it. The end of our story.*

*But what a story it was.*

*I see her face: my Angel, my killer, my salvation. Gray eyes locked with mine. No fear. No regret. Just love.*

*Just us.*

*If you go, I follow.*

*If you fall, I fall.*

*Together.*

*Always.*

# NADIA

*I spent fifteen years as a ghost. Empty. Cold. Dead inside.*

*Then she made me alive.*

*And now, in this final moment, with her hand in mine and her eyes on mine, I understand.*

*This is what it means to be human.*

*To love so fiercely you'd die for it.*

*To choose your own ending.*

*To refuse to be anything less than whole, even if wholeness means destruction.*

*I love you, Kira.*

*With everything I am.*

*With everything...*

# Afterword

Thank you for reading Burn With Me.
If you made it to the end, you've witnessed something I've been carrying for a long time, a story about the kind of love that doesn't fit into redemption arcs or happy endings.

I know Nadia and Kira make choices that are difficult to witness. Some of you might have decided they went too far, and I respect that. These aren't characters everyone will root for. But for those who stayed, who followed them all the way to their final choice, thank you. Thank you for sitting with the discomfort, for allowing space for a love story that ends in tragedy but still matters.

I wrote this because I wanted to explore what happens when love becomes obsession, when two people see each other so completely that the rest of the world disappears. They're not aspirational. They're cautionary. But they're also deeply, painfully human.

The black dahlias throughout this story are about beauty in darkness, about leaving something behind that says "I was here, and I mattered." That's what they tried to do, in their own violent way.

I hope you found something in their story that resonated, even if it's just the reminder that love, real and consuming and dangerous, is one of the most powerful forces in the world. It can save us. It can destroy us. Sometimes it does both.
If you're struggling with anything this brought up, please reach out for support. And if their story broke your heart the way I intended, please consider leaving a review or telling someone about them. Legends live on in the people who remember them.

Thank you for reading.
Until Next time,
Tatum


P.S. - In my headcanon, there's a garden somewhere filled with black dahlias, where two women who loved too fiercely finally found peace. Whether you believe that is entirely up to you.

# Also by Tatum Vale

Under Contract Series
The Terms of Us

Burn With Me (Standalone)
A Sapphic Romantic Tragedy

# Also by T. Vale

Beautiful Ruin
Doubled

# About the Author

Tatum Vale writes queer romance where desire makes a mess and nobody gets to pretend it didn't.

Their stories blend sharp chemistry with emotional chaos, built on bad decisions, close calls, and tension that bites back. Writing MM, sapphic, and polyamorous romances across multiple worlds, Tatum delivers connection that escalates, collides, and leaves marks.

When not writing, Tatum lives in late nights, loud feelings, and curiosity that doesn't behave.

Stalk Tatum's links via their website:
https://www.tatumvale.com/

www.ingramcontent.com/pod-product-compliance
Lightning Source LLC
Chambersburg PA
CBHW021129070726
47591CB00014B/1864